Samuel French Acting Edition

Thespian Playworks 2016

I Love Ruthie
by Adam Mirajkar

Lost and Found
by Alyssa Faykus

The Third Wall
by Kim Wong

Penelope
by Phanesia Pharel

FOR PRODUCTION ENQUIRIES

UNITED STATES AND CANADA
Info@SamuelFrench.com
1-866-598-8449

UNITED KINGDOM AND EUROPE
Plays@SamuelFrench.co.uk
020-7255-4302

Each title is subject to availability from Samuel French, depending upon country of performance. Please be aware that *THESPIAN PLAYWORKS 2016* may not be licensed by Samuel French in your territory. Professional and amateur producers should contact the nearest Samuel French office or licensing partner to verify availability.

No one shall make any changes in this title(s) for the purpose of production. No part of this book may be reproduced, stored in a retrieval system, or transmitted in any form, by any means, now known or yet to be invented, including mechanical, electronic, photocopying, recording, videotaping, or otherwise, without the prior written permission of the publisher. No one shall upload this title(s), or part of this title(s), to any social media websites.

For all enquiries regarding motion picture, television, and other media rights, please contact Samuel French.

MUSIC USE NOTE

Licensees are solely responsible for obtaining formal written permission from copyright owners to use copyrighted music in the performance of this play and are strongly cautioned to do so. If no such permission is obtained by the licensee, then the licensee must use only original music that the licensee owns and controls. Licensees are solely responsible and liable for all music clearances and shall indemnify the copyright owners of the play(s) and their licensing agent, Samuel French, against any costs, expenses, losses and liabilities arising from the use of music by licensees. Please contact the appropriate music licensing authority in your territory for the rights to any incidental music.

IMPORTANT BILLING AND CREDIT REQUIREMENTS

If you have obtained performance rights to this title, please refer to your licensing agreement for important billing and credit requirements.

ABOUT THESPIAN PLAYWORKS

Thespian Playworks is a writing contest and script-development program for high school students, sponsored by the Educational Theatre Association and run by the staff of *Dramatics* magazine. Each year, up to four finalists are invited to the International Thespian Festival in Lincoln, Nebraska, where the students work with a professional director, a dramaturg, and a volunteer cast of actors to put their short plays on their feet before a live audience.

Launched in 1994 as a tribute to longtime International Thespian Society executive Doug Finney, the program aims to nurture young playwrights, and over Playworks' history, many participants have gone on to college majors and careers in theatre, writing, and related fields. Whatever the eventual future of the writers or their scripts, Playworks is an exhilarating experience in a creative discipline seldom taught in schools or celebrated in the wider culture.

The call for entries goes out each fall, with submission deadlines in mid-winter. *Dramatics* receives scores of scripts from high school Thespians all over the U.S., Canada, and as far away as the United Arab Emirates. Each play is reviewed at least twice, as teams of readers (including *Dramatics* staff and other professional critics and theatre artists) narrow down the entries: first to a dozen semifinalists, then to the final four. Each semifinalist receives a personal letter with feedback on his or her script.

For more on Thespian Playworks, please visit www.edta.org/playworks.

CONTENTS

I Love Ruthie...7

Lost and Found 33

The Third Wall 65

Penelope 87

I Love Ruthie

Adam Mirajkar

I Love Ruthie, by Adam Mirajkar of Troupe 5742 at Blake High School, Apollo Beach, Florida, was presented in a staged reading as part of the Thespian Playworks program at the 2016 Thespian Festival on June 24. Phillip Moss was director, Dominic Orlando served as dramaturg, and Meghan Emanuel served as stage manager. The cast was as follows:

JACLYN	Ember Johnston
RUTHIE	Christen Carter
JOE	Zachary Bane
MIKE	Matthew Limas
MOM	Kat Andrews
DAD	Mike Nalley

CHARACTERS

JACLYN GOLDING – Thirteen. Went into a coma at age eight; five years later, she wakes up and finds she's been replaced by a girl her parents have adopted: Ruthie.

RUTHIE GOLDING – Thirteen. Proper, polite, and a manipulative snake.

JOE GOLDING – Seventeen. Kinda dumb and indifferent since he was never the family favorite anyway.

MIKE GOLDING – Eight. Kind of whiny, and a devotee of flag football who dreams of playing in the NFL (which will never happen). His memories have been twisted by Ruthie.

RALPH GOLDING (DAD) – Over-emotional, dopey dad.

ADAIRE GOLDING (MOM) – She runs the house; 1950s mom.

SETTING

The Golding household

AUTHOR'S NOTES

Keep it snappy and playful. In general, an en dash (–) indicates an interruption: a sudden shift in thought or action mid-line, or at the end of a line, another character cutting in. Ellipses (...) indicate more of a trailing off or loaded hesitation.

Scene One

*(A girl's room. It was originally **JACLYN**'s, but has been vastly redecorated. At center, **JACLYN** lies in the small bed with her family around her. **MOM**, **DAD**, **JOE**, and **MIKE** are going through their morning routine of bending her joints. **RUTHIE**, a proper girl with pigtails, is playing to the side with Mr. Piggy, a stuffed pink elephant.)*

DAD. So Mike, how's school going?

MIKE. It's okay…

DAD. And you, Joe?

JOE. It's alright. *(Pause.)* I'm actually tutoring Mike.

> *(**MOM** and **DAD** look at each other in fear, dropping **JACLYN**'s limbs for a brief, stunned second.)*

MOM. *(Panicked.)* Not math though, right –? *(Beat.)* Oh, Jaclyn, why do you have to –

> *(They all look down at the puddle that has formed.)*

Drool…

JOE. Gross. Can't you just stuff her mouth with toilet paper?

DAD. *(Sighs.)* I'll go get the mop.

> *(He exits to fetch the mop.)*

MIKE. Why does she have to drool so much?

MOM. She's been comatose for half a decade – it has to go somewhere.

> *(Noises of falling items echo from offstage, as **DAD** is trying to find what he needs. Sound from a televised football game is heard; **DAD** has been distracted.)*

God, he can't do anything right –

> (**MOM** *exits to find what kind of mess he's made. Hearing the football game,* **JOE** *and* **MIKE** *look at each other, then* **JACLYN***, at each other, then to the sound of the game, and then at each other.*)

JOE. I feel a little bad… I wanna stay…but the game's on…

MIKE. And it's one of the playoffs…

> (*The dilemma is killing* **JOE** *and* **MIKE***. They look at each other nervously, hoping one will suggest what the other can't.*)

JOE. (*Finally surrendering.*) Yeah, you're right!

> (**JOE** *and* **MIKE** *drop their sister's limbs and run off to the TV room.* **RUTHIE** *now sits alone with* **JACLYN***.*)

RUTHIE. I guess it's just you and me, pal.

> (**RUTHIE** *begins taking selfies with* **JACLYN***, making inappropriate and offensive gestures toward her. After she tires of that, she lightly knocks on her skull.* **JACLYN** *flutters awake slowly, to a slight look of malicious surprise from* **RUTHIE***, and gazes at her old room, which has been severely redecorated by* **RUTHIE***.*)

And the sleeping giant has awoken.

JACLYN. (*Pause.*) Who're you?

RUTHIE. (*Calling.*) Daddy – Mommy – she's awake!

JACLYN. Mom –? Dad –?

RUTHIE. Parents? The ones who, for whatever reason, chose not to terminate you as a fetus? You didn't think you came from a stork, did you?

JACLYN. No…no, I didn't… I just…is this my room?

RUTHIE. No. This is my room – but I'm sure Mom and Dad can refurbish the old doghouse in the back for you. I'm Ruthie. Ruthie Golding. I'm fairly good with pleasantries…if I care enough…

JACLYN. Hey… Golding…that's my last name. Are we related?

RUTHIE. I guess, if you're done being a drama queen.

JACLYN. What?

RUTHIE. *(Mocking.)* "Look at me – poor me, I'm unconscious – watch me sleep and drool."

*(**MOM** and **DAD** return.)*

MOM. Jaclyn… Oh my god, you're awake!

DAD. Sweetie…it's us… Don't you remember?

MOM. It has been five years, Ralph…

JACLYN. *(Pause.)* You guys look older. And bigger.

MOM. Your father traded out the gym for the couch and pigskins, but it's still us, honey!

(They hug and savor the moment. Aww.)

DAD. We should probably let Dr. Kahn know.

MOM. You choose now to do something about your lifestyle?

DAD. I meant Jaclyn –

*(Hearing **JACLYN**'s name, **MIKE** and **JOE** run over and enter, leaving the football game on, the sound remaining in the background.)*

JOE. Jaclyn?

*(The family joyfully begins to catch up with her, leaving **RUTHIE** to herself, while she looks out to the audience.)*

RUTHIE. In the flesh. For now…

Scene Two

*(Characters enter and exit into the living room
from other rooms in the house like a carousel.)*

MOM. Who dumped all the laundry out? I just folded it!

RUTHIE. I think I saw Jaclyn do it.

MOM. What? Why?

RUTHIE. Organized laundry's too fascist for some, I'd
imagine.

*(**MOM** exits and **DAD** enters.)*

DAD. Where's Goldie?

RUTHIE. I think I saw Jaclyn flushing him down the toilet.

DAD. Goldie…? He's gone…?

*(**DAD** exits crying and **JOE** enters.)*

JOE. Dude, what happened to that pile of laundry in my
room?

RUTHIE. The one that was growling? I'm surprised the
CDC hadn't quarantined your room yet. Jaclyn put it
in the wash –

JOE. THE WASH?! Why? They were clean!

RUTHIE. Joe.

JOE. Okay, semi-clean.

RUTHIE. Joe.

JOE. Half of semi-clean.

RUTHIE. They literally looked like you went scuba diving in
Chernobyl Lake. She had to use a whole container of
bleach. And it caught fire.

JOE. Oh my god…she burned my clothes…the little
arsonist!

*(**JOE** runs and exits, **MIKE** enters.)*

MIKE. Ruthie! Someone deflated my football!

RUTHIE. Oh no…

MIKE. I know right? What kind of person does that?

RUTHIE. Someone named Jaclyn. She told me she wants to outlaw football when she grows up. Says it causes brain damage.

>(**MIKE** *laughs as if it's the funniest joke he's heard, then goes silent when the grave realization washes over him.*)

MIKE. You're serious…what kinda hocus pocus is that? That's our family game!

RUTHIE. See, your non-biological sister would never do something like that to our family.

>(**MOM** *follows* **JACLYN** *into the living room, chastising her, and other members of the family come out from other rooms.*)

MOM. I can't believe you, Jaclyn – after everything we've done!

MIKE. Yeah, I've had to miss morning cartoons wiggling your paws and feet!

JACLYN. So, what'd I miss in the latest episode of *I Love Ruthie*…?

JOE. My laundry!

MIKE. My football!

DAD. Goldie!

JACLYN. Who –? Wow, I need to catch up. Anyone DVR it?

MIKE. This isn't some joke; these are egregious crimes –

MOM. Good word, honey!

DAD. *(Emotional.)* Proud of ya, son.

JOE. Outstanding – what's it mean?

>(*Everyone ignores* **JOE,** *and* **MIKE** *plows on as if he had never been interrupted.*)

MIKE. Crimes you committed!

>(**JACLYN** *looks behind her as if someone else must be under accusation, then turns to the family, surprised.*)

DAD, MOM, MIKE & JOE. You!

JACLYN. I didn't do anything!

MIKE. So you're saying Ruthie's lying? She would just make all this up?

JOE. Ruthie would never lie!

MOM. What a sacrilegious thing to say.

DAD. Heresy.

JACLYN. I swear – I didn't do anything!

RUTHIE. Jaclyn… It's okay… We understand you want attention. Not like you haven't gotten it for the past five years…

DAD. You don't have to lash out like this.

JACLYN. I didn't –

MIKE. You just hate football, don't you?

JOE. And other people's clothes.

MOM. Joe…that was a health hazard.

DAD. What did you have against Goldie? *(Pause.)* He was just a beta.

JACLYN. I never even –

DAD. Did you have candles, or a eulogy?

JACLYN. Dad, I didn't –

DAD. Oh god…

JACLYN. Dad, I didn't even do anything –

> (**DAD** *sobs uncontrollably.*)

DAD. That's it, you're grounded! Go to your room – now!

> (**JACLYN**, *beyond shocked, exits to her room, with* **RUTHIE** *smirking triumphantly.*)

MOM. *(Consoling* **DAD**.*)* C'mon, I'll take you to Juanita's Jumbo Jelly Jamboree, and we'll get ice cream, okay, Pookie Pie?

> (**DAD** *continues sobbing, and* **MOM** *and* **DAD** *exit through the front door.* **RUTHIE** *laughs, and with a flourish, spins.*)

Scene Three

(Parents have left. JOE, MIKE, RUTHIE, and JACLYN are home alone. JOE and MIKE are sitting on the couch, watching football. JACLYN enters looking for Mr. Piggy.)

JACLYN. Have either of you seen Mr. Piggy?

JOE. We're busy. Go away, laundry murderer.

JACLYN. Call me all the names you want, but you weren't too busy earlier when you snuck your girlfriend over. Can't wait to give Mom and Dad that little detail when they get back.

JOE. *(Tries to get up.)* Huh? Wait, Jaclyn –

(JACLYN exits to her room.)

JACLYN. Oh no, you're busy, don't worry about it…

MIKE. Sit down, he's about to make the next play!

(RUTHIE enters with Mr. Piggy. She stands disapprovingly, then grabs the remote and changes it to her favorite TV show.)

JOE. What the hell?

MIKE. We were watching that!

RUTHIE. Joseph, do not use that kind of language towards me!

JOE. Ruthie, for the last time – don't call me that. Besides, what are you going to do about it?

RUTHIE. I am going to tell Mom and Dad about your impolite behavior when they come home.

JOE. Jesus, just go back to the game.

(JOE reaches to RUTHIE for the remote. She swats him away.)

RUTHIE. Joe!

MIKE. Ruthie, we're about to win!

RUTHIE. Heavens no, all you boys need is more violence.

(JACLYN has come in and watches from behind.)

JACLYN. What if I want to watch football, too – it's my favorite. Hey – that's Mr. Piggy!

RUTHIE. Porky is mine.

JACLYN. His name isn't Porky! It's Mr. Piggy.

(They start tugging at Mr. Piggy.)

MIKE. I thought it was Porky?

JOE. Can you guys stop…

JACLYN. Give him back to me!

RUTHIE. Porky is not yours, he's mine!

JACLYN. No, he's not!

RUTHIE. Yes, he is!

JACLYN. Mr. Piggy's mine! You mad sis, that they aren't your real parents?

(Pause.)

RUTHIE. I beg your pardon?

JACLYN. They're not your real parents. They ain't your parents. You're adopted.

RUTHIE. Oh Jaclyn, really, "ain't" is so improper –

JACLYN. *(Interjects.)* It's in the dictionary.

RUTHIE. And grammatically incorrect.

JACLYN. I don't care! They're not yours! Somebody just dumped you in a little take-out box on our doorstep!

RUTHIE. *(Laughs.)* Oh Jaclyn… You're just jealous that they love me more. Mike and Joe love me more too, right?

JOE. Don't drag me into this.

RUTHIE. I was a better fit to this family in five years than you ever were in your entire life.

MIKE. Can we just go back to the game?

RUTHIE. That sucks, doesn't it? Waking up looking different than you did when you fell asleep. Think of all the things you missed – all the memories, your friends… By the way, Roger? You remember Roger Brown? I kissed him.

JACLYN. Ew – that's gross, boys have cooties!

RUTHIE. Do they though? I guess you wouldn't know.

JACLYN. You evil, stupid –

MIKE. Stupid isn't a nice word, Jaclyn. That's gonna be ten cents in the swear jar.

RUTHIE. See, Mike? She goes into a coma and just blames anybody for anything. *(To* JACLYN.*)* Do you even know what a coma is?

JACLYN. *(Proud.)* It's a type of punctuation. Even I remember that from school.

RUTHIE. Wrong. It is "the state of unconsciousness in which the person cannot be awakened, nor respond to light."

JACLYN. That's what I said!

RUTHIE. Shut up. Just admit that I've been more of a sister than you ever have. Michael, do you even remember Jaclyn before she went to sleep? Of course not –

JACLYN. He was like, five –

RUTHIE. Michael doesn't remember you. There's nothing to remember.

JACLYN. *(To* MIKE.*)* Don't you remember when we got ice cream and it melted all over your shirt? And Mom wasn't going to get you a new one, so I saved up and bought you the exact same one? You told – you hugged me, and said I was the best big sis in the world.

MIKE. …Sure, I remember Ruthie saved up for that shirt.

JACLYN. What –? No, that's not –

RUTHIE. Truth hurts, doesn't it Jaclyn? Mike, your memory is correct: we did get cookies 'n cream and cake batter.

JACLYN. That's what we got! And the cake batter had sprinkles on it? Mike, she's lying to you, it was me who was there, not her. I swear, Mike, how could you forget?

MIKE. Jaclyn stop, you're freaking me out. You've been sleeping all this time; you couldn't have –

RUTHIE. Michael, she's delusional. It's the side effects from her little nap kicking in – don't be scared. I won't let anything bad happen to you.

JACLYN. Mike, Ruthie's manipulating you!

RUTHIE. Are you just jelly that Michael loves me more? That Mr. Piggy loves me more? That your parents love me more? That your life loves me more than you? You're just a loveless loser.

(JACLYN *lunges at* RUTHIE.)

JACLYN. I hate you – you stupid –

(MIKE *gasps and covers his ears.*)

MIKE. Twenty cents!

JOE. Jaclyn!

(JACLYN *tackles* RUTHIE *to the floor, clawing away at her face, while* RUTHIE *tries hitting* JACLYN, *and using Mr. Piggy as a shield.* MIKE *is starting to cry, and* JOE *stands up to take action – but does nothing.*)

RUTHIE. Help me! She's trying to kill me – she's trying to kill your sister.

JACLYN. No, I'm the real one!

RUTHIE. No you're not – I am!

(JACLYN *takes Mr. Piggy and begins using it to suffocate* RUTHIE. *After a struggle,* RUTHIE *dies. Pause.*)

JOE. You killed her.

JACLYN. I didn't mean to… I just wanted to put her to sleep.

MIKE. A nap doesn't last forever.

JACLYN. Oh no…what are Mom and Dad going to say?

JOE. They're going to kill us – they're going to kill you.

JACLYN. I just wanted them to love me again.

JOE. Good luck after this.

JACLYN. She started it!

MIKE. You started it by waking up!

JOE. Jaclyn…what are we going to do? What are you going to do?

JACLYN. You saw – you did nothing. You just stood there!

JOE. I couldn't –

JACLYN. You could've pulled me off, you're stronger than me. I just got out of a coma, you're just as guilty as me –

JOE. Are you insane?

MIKE. Is that even a question.

JACLYN. *(To* JOE.*)* I'm telling Mom and Dad about you bringing over your girly friend while they're gone.

MIKE. You're the one who murdered her!

JACLYN. I didn't mean to!

MIKE. Did too!

JACLYN. Did not!

MIKE. Did too!

JOE. Guys, shut up! What are we going to do?

MIKE. You're helping her?

JOE. She's blackmailing me!

JACLYN. You deserve it!

MIKE. I hate you both! I'm…I'm going to call Mom and Dad.

> (**MIKE** *moves toward the phone, but* **JACLYN** *dives and grabs his leg.)*

JACLYN. Mike please, I swear, I'll do whatever you want – just don't tell them. I'll be your slave for a month – I'll do your chores, anything!

> (**MIKE** *pauses, considering.)*

MIKE. I want your portion of dessert for a month –

JACLYN. A month?

MIKE. And I want your weekly allowance for the next…let's say…two months.

JACLYN. Two months?!

MIKE. Football cards ain't cheap, lady.

JACLYN. Okay – sure, fine –

MIKE. And I want half up-front.

JACLYN. Half up-front? But, I don't –

MIKE. Should've thought about that before you went around killing sisters.

JACLYN. Ugh – okay, fine, I'll get it to you tonight. I promise.

(**MIKE** *looks at her, then smirks at* **JOE**.)

MIKE. Touchdown.

JACLYN. But you better not snitch.

MIKE. I won't.

(*The three of them look at the body.*)

JOE. We could tell them she ran away?

JACLYN. They'd believe that, right? And then I could be the daughter that stays with them sticks with them, and they'd love me…

JOE. …But where would we put her?

(*Pause. They look back at* **RUTHIE** *again.* **JOE** *begins to pace, like a detective.*)

MIKE. She was so happy here, why'd you have to take that away? God, you ruin everything.

JOE. Not behind the couch –

JACLYN. (*To* **MIKE**.) Please hug me –

JOE. Maybe in the backyard –?

MIKE. (*To* **JACLYN**.) Ew, no. I already took a bath today, Jaclyn the Ripper. Hug Joe.

JACLYN. Um, no thanks.

JOE. What is everyone's problem with my hygiene?

(**MIKE** *and* **JACLYN** *look at* **JOE**, *each other, then at* **JOE**.)

JACLYN & MIKE. Keep thinking!

JOE. Fine! Sheesh…could bury her near the rose bushes…

MIKE. (*Moving away from* **JACLYN**.) Just leave me alone.

JOE. No… Mom gardens there every day…not sure she'd appreciate her dead kid beneath the weeds.

JACLYN. Mike, please –

JOE. Least the soil'd be more fertile.

> (*Car doors are heard slamming offstage. The parents are back.*)

JACLYN. Oh my god, they're home.

MIKE. Oooooh, you're going to be in so much trouble.

JACLYN. Joe what do we do –?

JOE. I'm thinking, I'm thinking!

MIKE. Joe, don't help her!

JACLYN. (*To* MIKE.) I'm giving you my dessert and allowance!

MIKE. So? I can still play devil's advocate!

JOE. Um…how about the closet?

MIKE. Joe! That's my place!

> (*Voices are heard offstage. The parents are near the door.*)

JACLYN. Joe, put her there!

> (JOE *goes to the body and starts to pick it up, expecting assistance. He doesn't get any.*)

JOE. Is anybody going to help? She's heavier than she looks.

MIKE. I thought you weren't supposed to talk about a woman's weight.

JACLYN. Ew, I don't want to touch her…she's dead.

MIKE. Wow, wonder how she got that way.

JOE. C'mon, just help me!

> (*The kids drag* RUTHIE *to the closet and prop her, standing up, inside. The closet opens in a way so the audience can see, but the parents can't from their position in the living room. The front door rattles just as they close the closet door, and the kids drape themselves over furniture as if they haven't moved a muscle; trying way too hard to appear nonchalant and well-behaved.*)

MOM. Hey kids.

JACLYN. Hey Mom.

DAD. How was the game?

JOE. Brutal.

MOM. Your father and I –

DAD. Where's Ruthie?

MOM. Yes, where is she?

>   *(The kids look at each other, but **MIKE** beats them to it.)*

MIKE. She's dead.

>   *(**JOE** tries to put his hand over **MIKE**'s mouth.)*

DAD. Michael! How could you say such an awful thing?

JOE. He's kidding, Dad.

MOM. Jaclyn, is that some twisted joke you told him?

JACLYN. No? Why would I –?

MOM. Can you explain anything you do?

JACLYN. Puberty?

JOE. Ruthie's sleeping – she went to bed early tonight.

DAD. Oh. I guess it is late. You kids should follow her example, and hop to it.

>   *(He begins taking off his coat and heads to the closet.)*

JOE. Let me get that for you, Pops.

>   *(**JOE** puts his hand on the coat.)*

DAD. That's alright Joe, don't stress yourself out now.

JOE. No, really Dad.

>   *(Tense pause.)*

MOM. Oh, just let him.

DAD. If you insist…

>   *(**JOE** takes the coat and heads to the closet.)*

JACLYN. Soooo… How was your evening?

MOM. Wonderful. Mike…you look like you've seen a ghost. I hope you kids didn't watch anything scary on TV.

(**JOE** *turns to look, and as he does,* **RUTHIE***'s body falls on top of him – but the open door obscures the body from parental view.* **JACLYN** *looks at* **MIKE***, and when the parents aren't looking at her, mimes cutting her throat.*)

MIKE. …I'm just…tired.

DAD. Go get some shut-eye then.

(*From this angle, they can't see that it's a body on top of* **JOE***; they just think it's some fallen object from the closet.*)

MOM. Joe, do you need some help?

JOE. No, I got it –!

DAD. It's that dratted vacuum and all those mops you shoved in there.

MOM. Ralph – stop squawking and go help him.

JACLYN. That's okay – I'll do it!

MOM. (*Pause.*) Wow…we go away for the night and our children become good Samaritans.

(**MOM** *exits.*)

MIKE. Not really –

DAD. Looks like you're finally starting to adjust, Jaclyn.

(**JACLYN** *and* **JOE** *finally shove the body back in.*)

JACLYN. I'm trying.

DAD. You think Ruthie might want a bedtime story?

JOE & JACLYN. NO!

DAD. …Why not?

JACLYN. Oh…you shouldn't bother her… She was really tired –

MIKE. You can't bother her because –

JOE. Nah, let her sleep. You know cranky she gets.

(*Pause.*)

DAD. Ruthie cranky? Malarkey.

JACLYN. Trust me, she does.

MIKE. You're one to talk –

DAD. What is with you kids? You're acting like savages.

JACLYN. Nothing, we – why don't you read us a story?

DAD. I'm busy, Jaclyn.

(**DAD** *exits.*)

MOM. *(Offstage.)* Ralph! Ralph? Your fish tank's leaking again, you need to get a mop – Ralph?

JACLYN. *(A stage hiss.)* Mike! I gave you my dessert and my allowance for the next two months –

MIKE. Three months of allowance and dessert or I squeal.

JACLYN. Three months?!

MOM. *(Offstage, but closer.)* Ralph?

JACLYN. Urgh! Fine – but you better not tell.

(**MOM** *enters.*)

MOM. Tell what?

(*Pause.*)

JACLYN. We...wanted to tell you...that Dad's...in your room!

(*Pause.*)

MOM. Well, his stupid fish tank is leaking all over my nice linoleum.

JOE. You want me to go get him?

MOM. Who? Your father? Hah! I'll just mop it.

JACLYN. No! Um –

MOM. Jaclyn, you're really stressing me out tonight.

(**MOM** *crosses to the closet.*)

MIKE. She's acting like that because –

JACLYN. *(Glaring at* **MIKE**.*)* The mop is not in the closet.

MOM. That's a load of hooey, I just put it there this morning –

JACLYN. It got moved.

MOM. Moved? Why...?

JOE. Yeah – to the kitchen.

MIKE. Kitchen?

JACLYN. Kitchen.

MOM. Kitchen? Did you kids spill something…

JACLYN. No – we figured the tank might leak again.

MOM. Oh…well…that was…semi-thoughtful of you. I didn't see it there, though.

JOE. It should be there. By the oven.

> *(**MOM** exits. **JACLYN** and **JOE** run to the closet to try and grab the mop while balancing the body. **MIKE** begins to exit.)*

MIKE. Your little game's over –

JACLYN. You promised –!

MIKE. I'm eight years old – my word doesn't mean squat! Mo-o-o-o-o-om!

> *(As he's yelling, **JACLYN** and **JOE** open the closet door to grab the mop, and the body falls on them.)*

JACLYN. Grab him!

> *(**JOE** runs to try and grab **MIKE**, while **JACLYN** struggles holding up the body, trying to retrieve the mop. **MOM** enters and **JACLYN** shuts the door just in time, but **RUTHIE**'s arm is sticking out. **JACLYN** positions herself, as if she's casually leaning up against the door, putting the mop in **RUTHIE**'s hand so that it looks like **JACLYN**'s. **JOE** has grabbed **MIKE** in a hug, and **MOM** enters, going to grab the mop, but when she accepts it she turns to address the boys, not paying too much attention to the awkward stiff hand.)*

MOM. *(Grabbing mop.)* Jaclyn, I told you it was in the clos– Jesus! Your hands are freezing! Joe, Mike, in case you don't remember last time, if you're going to act like gorillas, the front door's that way.

JOE. Just showing some brotherly love.

(**MIKE** *is struggling, trying to remove* **JOE**'s *hand from over his mouth.* **DAD** *enters,* **MOM** *turns her attention to him, and* **JACLYN** *begins to deal with* **RUTHIE**'s *hand.*)

DAD. Are you guys still up –?

MOM. Ralph, where were you? I called and called!

DAD. I was in the bathroom. Honey, you know Mexican food and my bowels don't sing "La Bamba" after a meal.

(**MIKE** *can see the arm sticking out.*)

MOM. Well, the tank's leaking again –

MIKE. *(Getting* **JOE**'s *hand off.)* Mom – look!

MOM. Michael, do not interrupt when I'm having a conversation; it's rude. You'll have to wait your turn.

(**JACLYN** *struggles to stuff the arm back in the closet, while* **MIKE** *tries to get* **MOM**'s *attention.*)

DAD. The tank's leaking? I just flushed and everything's –

MIKE. B-b-b-b-but –

MOM. The fish tank! *(Turning to scold.)* Michael…

DAD. Oh, that one…did you get the mop?

MOM. No, don't you know? The mop look is so "in," according to *Cosmopolitan.*

DAD. So…you already mopped it?

MOM. *(Throws mop at him)* God, Ralph, you're infuriating.

(**MOM** *starts to exit, much to* **MIKE**'s *dismay.*)

MIKE. Mom – look!

MOM. What?

MIKE. The closet!

(*Everyone looks at the closet, which appears perfectly normal at this point.*)

MOM. Yes… I see the closet too…

MIKE. But…but – there was a –

(**MOM** *leaves, clearly having better things to do.*)

DAD. Enough games and stuttering, Mike, off to bed.

MIKE. But Dad, I have to tell you –

DAD. It can wait till morning –

MIKE. No, it's important –

DAD. Michael. It can wait till morning. *(Inspecting mop.)* Now… Where's the better one, is it in the closet?

JACLYN. Better one…?

DAD. Yeah, the other mop has a flatter head and soaks up more.

JOE. It broke.

JACLYN. Snapped in two.

MIKE. Dad –

DAD. Michael, not another word! It couldn't have, I just used it earlier.

> *(He moves toward the closet.)*

JACLYN. It's not there, I swear –

DAD. Jaclyn…I'm pretty sure it is.

> *(**DAD** opens the closet, and **RUTHIE** falls onto him.)*

What are you doing out of bed –? Oh…oh god… you're…dead. *(Turns to kids.)* Someone's in big trouble!

> *(All the kids point fingers at each other.)*

JOE, MIKE & JACLYN. Wasn't me!

Scene Four

*(JACLYN's room. This time nothing of **RUTHIE**'s exists, and **JACLYN** is comatose on the bed, hooked up to a quietly beeping heart monitor, with **MOM**, **DAD**, **MIKE**, and **JOE** looking at her.)*

MOM. God, I wish this just could be over.

DAD. Me too dear, me too.

JOE. She looks so peaceful.

MIKE. C'mon sis, just snap out of it – oh, why won't she wake up?

DAD. Mike…sometimes these things just take time.

MIKE. But – how long? How long will it take?

DAD. I'm not sure, son. I'm not sure.

MOM. We should go. Give her space.

DAD. Maybe we should tell Dr. Kahn to –

MOM. To what?

DAD. You know…

JOE. You mean take her off life support?

MIKE. Does that mean you're going to kill her?

MOM. Oh, Ralph…how can you even –

DAD. Adaire, we can't keep going on like this.

MIKE. *(Over-dramatic.)* Murderer!

*(**MIKE** faints, but no one cares, so he picks himself up.)*

MOM. Ralph…I just can't.

*(**MOM** exits sobbing, and **DAD** follows, trying to console her.)*

MIKE. Do you remember that time we got ice cream –

JOE. No, but you're probably going to tell me anyway.

MIKE. Well, I was wearing my favorite shirt, and we got cake batter and cookies 'n cream, and the cake batter had these little pink sprinkles all over – but then it melted all over my shirt. So, Jaclyn saved up and bought the exact same one for me. I just wish she was here.

JOE. *(Pause.)* C'mon. Let's go get some ice cream.

> (JOE *and* MIKE *exit.* RUTHIE *enters. Smiling at the audience, she grabs Mr. Piggy, places it over* JACLYN*'s mouth, and suffocates her. Lights dim and the heart monitor goes dead.)*

End of Play

Matthew Limas, Zachary Bane, Ember Johnston, and Christen Carter as rival siblings in the Thespian Festival staged reading of *I Love Ruthie,* by Adam Mirajkar.

Lost and Found

Alyssa Faykus

Lost and Found, by Alyssa Faykus of Troupe 1315 at Brenham (Texas) High School, was presented in a staged reading as part of the Thespian Playworks program at the 2016 Thespian Festival on June 25. Carolyn Cork Greer was director, Nicholas C. Pappas served as dramaturg, and Hilda Rey served as stage manager. The cast was as follows:

CLAIRE . . . . .Casey Durso

THOMAS/GEORGE . . . . .Jonathan Connolly

RYLIE . . . . .Elizabeth Miller

OWEN . . . . Paul Fico

CHARACTERS

THOMAS – A semi-magical being. Keeper of the Lost and Found, boisterous and quirky. He has been at the Lost and Found for one year.

CLAIRE – Around eighteen. She has lost something close to her heart. Independent by nature, she finds it very hard to ask for help.

RYLIE – Twenties. Very perky, slightly ditsy, just wants to help. Follows her heart. She lives at the Lost and Found but has a day job somewhere else. Is wearing an engagement ring.

OWEN – Twenties or thirties. Wise, knowledgeable, follows his head. A master's student in divinity, he's on a missionary assignment, though he is not an "in your face"-type Christian. Might have a Bible or wear a cross necklace.

GEORGE – Doubles as Thomas. Around eighteen, has depression, and has recently committed suicide. Dorky and geeky, but a big-hearted and lovely person. Key to Claire's happiness.

SETTING

A random building in New York City. At center, a desk with a high-backed office chair behind it that swivels around. To one side, a few chairs lined up as in a principal's office, or a couch as in a therapist's room. On the other side, a very large box labeled "Lost and Found" with miscellaneous objects in it.

(Lights up on the Lost and Found. **THOMAS** *is sitting in the desk chair, turned away and concealed behind the high back.* **CLAIRE** *enters carrying a small keepsake box with a little padlock on it.)*

CLAIRE. Hello? Hello? Anyone here? *(Reads plaque on desk.)* Thomas? *(Rings desk bell.)* Can I get some assistance please?

THOMAS. *(Swivels around in chair.)* HELLO!

CLAIRE. Ahh! You scared me!

THOMAS. That was the point. What can I help you with?

CLAIRE. Well I found this, *(Holds up the small box.)* and I was wondering if you could help me identify it?

THOMAS. Is it yours?

CLAIRE. No. I found it on my –

THOMAS. Well, then it goes into the box. *(He snatches the small box, crosses to the big box, and drops it in.)*

CLAIRE. Hey!

THOMAS. Is it yours?

CLAIRE. No, I *found* it, this morning.

THOMAS. That is exactly why I threw it in the box. This is the Lost and Found. I don't make the rules around here, I'm the dude who watches the box. So I take it that you are lost?

CLAIRE. What?

THOMAS. Well Claire, this isn't just some ordinary Lost and Found. It's for people.

CLAIRE. No, I found *that* on my front step this morning and thought maybe someone lost it.

THOMAS. You think someone lost something *on* your front step. No, no, no, no, no. The front step is where people put babies and kittens that turn into Disney movies, *not* random objects. So, I believe this *(He grabs the small box from the big box.)* actually does belong to you.

CLAIRE. It can't belong to me.

THOMAS. Why not?

CLAIRE. It doesn't.

THOMAS. I don't believe you.

CLAIRE. Well, you should.

THOMAS. I'm not gonna. Tell me. *(He sits in his chair.)*

CLAIRE. I already –

THOMAS. *(He begins spinning around in his chair.)* Tell me, tell me, tell me!

CLAIRE. I told you, it's not mine.

THOMAS. Tellllll meeeeeeee!! *(He gets out of his chair, falls to his knees, and begs* **CLAIRE.***)*

CLAIRE. It's my friend George's.

THOMAS. Okay, and why did you bring George's – uh… what is this thing?

CLAIRE. It's a box.

THOMAS. Why did you bring George's box here?

CLAIRE. There's a lock on the box so I can't open it. I didn't know what else to do with it.

THOMAS. Ahhh, so you *are* the one that's lost.

CLAIRE. I'm not lost.

THOMAS. Then why are you here with this box?

CLAIRE. I just thought –

THOMAS. That by getting rid of this box that George gave to you it would magically change the way you feel. That by giving *me* this box all of your pain would just be magically whisked away. Right?

CLAIRE. Right.

THOMAS. Wrong!

CLAIRE. Excuse me?

THOMAS. It's not going to change a thing.

CLAIRE. And why is that?

THOMAS. Because you still have an attachment to the guy.

CLAIRE. Wrong.

(He gives her a look.)

Okay, right. But this thing just meant so much to the both of us and the fact that I ended up with it just makes me feel…

THOMAS. Mad?

CLAIRE. No, more…

THOMAS. Sad.

CLAIRE. Yeah.

THOMAS. Well, it looks like you have come to just the right place!

CLAIRE. What?

THOMAS. The Lost and Found. The lost and found *box.* For people. People like you. Now Claire, get in the box.

CLAIRE. No thanks.

THOMAS. Oh, come on! What do you have to lose? You're already sad, I can't see anything else that could possibly make you feel any worse. Now, *(Slightly nudging her.)* get in the box.

CLAIRE. You're kind of rude, do you know that?

THOMAS. *(Grabs her shoulders, invading her space.)* Oh Claire, I'm not rude, just honest. *(He shoves her in the direction of the box.)*

CLAIRE. *(Hesitantly.)* Okay…here I go.

OWEN. OUCH! I was sleeping in here!

CLAIRE. Ahh! Why didn't you tell me there was someone else in here?

OWEN. Yeah, Thomas, why not? Man, I think that girl gave me a concussion.

CLAIRE. Oh, gosh I'm sorry. Here, let me help you up.

OWEN. No, no, no, I'll do it myself. *(He gets up.)* Phew, now that that's out of the way, I'm Owen, and you are?

CLAIRE. Claire. Sorry I kicked you.

OWEN. Oh it's alright. It's water under the bridge.

CLAIRE. So who are you?

OWEN. I'm the dude that sleeps in the box.

CLAIRE. And why do you do that?

OWEN. Well, because I'm lost, like you.

CLAIRE. I'm not lost.

OWEN. Okay, if you insist.

CLAIRE. *(Turns back to* THOMAS*.)* So Thomas, why am I in this box?

THOMAS. Well, Claire, sometimes this box is where people like to do their thinking –

OWEN. Or napping.

THOMAS. Yes, or napping. Though I prefer to use the box for thinking.

CLAIRE. Well what is there to think about?

THOMAS. Anything really. Boxes are great houses to the imagination. One can invent a peaceful meadow or a magic robot pirate island or even a new friend. *(He snaps his fingers and* RYLIE *pops out of the box.)*

RYLIE. Hiya!

CLAIRE. Ahh! What is up with you people and scaring me?!

RYLIE. It gets a little boring around here sometimes.

THOMAS & OWEN. Yeah.

CLAIRE. So the solution to your boredom is scaring the living daylights out of me?!

THOMAS, OWEN & RYLIE. Yeah.

CLAIRE. Okay. So what's your name?

RYLIE. Rylie! Nice to meet you. *(She hugs* CLAIRE*.)* And you are?

CLAIRE. Claire. Nice to meet you, too. So, Thomas, why am I in this box?

THOMAS. Well, because you're lost.

CLAIRE. I didn't think I was lost.

THOMAS. Then how did you end up here?

CLAIRE. I like to walk, you know, to get my mind off of things and I saw this place and I had never seen it before so I walked in and –

RYLIE, OWEN & THOMAS. Found us!

CLAIRE. Yeah.

RYLIE. It's because you were lost.

CLAIRE. No, I specifically remember I was on Travis Street.

OWEN. Claire, this has nothing to do with maps! This isn't the kind of lost that a GPS can fix.

RYLIE. It's okay, Claire. You're in a safe place. I know you're hurting.

OWEN. Rylie.

RYLIE. What? It's because of the "S" word.

OWEN & THOMAS. Rylie!

RYLIE. Sorry.

THOMAS. We're getting off-topic. So first off let's start with that friend of yours.

CLAIRE. I don't want to talk about it.

THOMAS. Secondly, we should talk about that denial problem of yours.

CLAIRE. I don't have a denial problem!

THOMAS. And obviously you have some unresolved anger issues, too.

CLAIRE. That's it, I'm getting out of here!

THOMAS. Freeze! *(Everyone stops moving for a second, but then* **CLAIRE** *begins to move.)* Ah, dang it!

CLAIRE. *(She begins heading for the door, but it's as if she is moving through molasses.)* I've had it with these silly games. All I wanted to do was get rid of this box and now all I want to do is get out. *(She realizes her legs are barely moving.)* Get out. Get out, get out! What's going on?

THOMAS. I hate to do this to you.

CLAIRE. Do what?

THOMAS. Well aren't you wondering why your legs are barely moving?

CLAIRE. Just a little bit.

THOMAS. It's simple really. I just want to talk to you about all of this.

CLAIRE. What did you do to my legs?!

THOMAS. Can we just talk?

CLAIRE. Yes. Let's start with my legs. What did you do?

THOMAS. Nothing.

CLAIRE. You tell me right now.

THOMAS. Do you trust me?

CLAIRE. No!

THOMAS. Then I can't tell you.

RYLIE. Claire, just trust him.

CLAIRE. Why should I trust him? I barely know him.

OWEN. Thomas, I think it's time.

CLAIRE. Time for what?

THOMAS. Are you sure?

(**OWEN** *nods his head.*)

Okay then. Claire, if I answer three questions about your life correctly, will you trust me?

CLAIRE. Do I get to pick the questions?

THOMAS. Within reason, yes. Think of three of your favorite things. Got them?

CLAIRE. Yes.

THOMAS. Okay, first question.

CLAIRE. What's my favorite color?

THOMAS. Say it on three. One, two, three:

CLAIRE & THOMAS. Turquoise.

CLAIRE. Okay, my favorite band.

THOMAS. One, two, three:

THOMAS & CLAIRE. Good Charlotte.

CLAIRE. My favorite ice cream flavor.

THOMAS. One, two, three:

CLAIRE & THOMAS. Pistachio.

RYLIE. Ew, that's gross.

THOMAS. I got them all right.

CLAIRE. Okay, I'll trust you. I'm really freaked out but I'll trust you.

THOMAS. Okay, great! Quicksand.

CLAIRE. What?

THOMAS. Your feet, I put a quicksand spell on them.

CLAIRE. So you're a wizard?

THOMAS. No, I'm just magic.

CLAIRE. I don't believe you.

THOMAS. Ah, but you trust me.

CLAIRE. I want out!

THOMAS. *(In a sing-song voice.)* The only way out is if you talk about it!

CLAIRE. You know you can talk to me without all the silly business.

THOMAS. But the silly business is how I get you to talk to me.

CLAIRE. No, not really.

THOMAS. Well you see, now I have something that you want.

CLAIRE. And what's that?

THOMAS. Freedom.

CLAIRE. Well, yeah, I don't really like to be held against my will.

THOMAS. That's not the kind of freedom I'm talking about. You see, the kind of freedom you're seeking isn't going to come from being let out of this room. The kind of freedom you are seeking is in you. And until you realize that, you aren't going to go anywhere. It's like you're trapped in, oh I dunno, QUICKSAAAAAND?!

CLAIRE. Thomas, this is crazy!

OWEN. But it's true.

RYLIE. Yeah. I mean, look at us. We've been here for a while now and it's all for one reason.

OWEN. We can't let go of the past.

RYLIE. And until we do…

OWEN. We'll be stuck here.

RYLIE. *(Over-dramatically.)* Forever.

CLAIRE. I don't see what this has to do with me, I'm fine.

THOMAS. No, you're not.

CLAIRE. Why do you even care?

THOMAS. Because you found me. This is the Lost and Found. Lost. *(Points to* **CLAIRE.***)* Found. *(Points to himself.)* I am only trying to help you. What you brought to me today was a thing, and what I'm offering you is a solution.

CLAIRE. I never even asked for your help!

THOMAS. Yes you did.

CLAIRE. When?

THOMAS. I believe your exact words were, ahem, *(Mimicking her voice.)* "Well I found this weird thing and I was wondering if you could help me identify it?" That thing, this thing *(Holds up the box.)* is all of your problems. And by handing me this box you gave me all of your problems. And I am going to fix them.

CLAIRE. Why would you do that?

THOMAS. Because once upon a time, just like you I stumbled upon this little place. I haven't left since I got here, and besides, I think that there is someone that needs your company just a little bit more than I do.

CLAIRE. And who is that?

THOMAS. We both know the answer to that question Claire.

CLAIRE. George?

THOMAS. Why are you so surprised?

CLAIRE. I don't want to talk about it.

THOMAS. Claire, the only way that you are ever going to get out of here is if you talk to me. I'm only trying to help.

CLAIRE. Well then can you free my legs?

THOMAS. And how would that help? Only you can set yourself free. And besides, all things considered I'm surprised you didn't run away sooner.

RYLIE. We do seem a little bit crazy.

OWEN. Yeah, Thomas, you are kinda weird.

THOMAS. I'm not weird. *(Angrily whispers to* OWEN *and* RYLIE*:)* You guys aren't helping me out here.

CLAIRE. I won't leave. Promise. You guys are *all* really weird but I feel like there's something I need.

RYLIE. Oh, guys I think she's gonna say it!

CLAIRE. It's –

THOMAS. Quicksand, quicksand, quicksand!!

CLAIRE. Because I need help!

THOMAS. Ding ding ding ding! Woo woo woo!! YEEEESS!!

> *(A gameshow effect: confetti falls, lights go crazy, and* **THOMAS** *furiously hits the bell on his desk.* **RYLIE** *throws glitter in the air and begins making snow angels in it, exclaiming "I love glitter. Yay!" etc.)*

CLAIRE. What the –?!

OWEN. Congratulations!

RYLIE. You have just completed step one!

> *(***OWEN** *holds up a large sign that says "Step One: Complete.")*

CLAIRE. Step one? Step one of what?

OWEN. Thomas, show the lady!

THOMAS. Rylie, please!

> *(***RYLIE** *struggles to pick up a big book from the Lost and Found and hands it to* **THOMAS**. *To him it is as light as a feather.)*

RYLIE. Here you go!

CLAIRE. What is that?

THOMAS. This, my dear Claire, is the Lost and Found Manual. These are the guidelines that we must follow in order to achieve successful freedom.

CLAIRE. Okay, and step one is?

RYLIE. Step one is admitting you need help.

OWEN. Congratulations!

CLAIRE. Why are you congratulating me? Why is this such a big deal?

THOMAS. Claire, try moving your feet.

CLAIRE. *(She is able to lift her feet but still can't move much.)* Hey! Look at that!

THOMAS. Now, I have not yet fully lifted the quicksand spell, but you are, and no pun intended, one STEP closer to your goal!

OWEN. Boo.

RYLIE. Hiss.

THOMAS. Ah, come on guys! Puns are great!

OWEN. The last time I checked there are no puns in the manual.

RYLIE. Oh darn, looks like you can't make any more.

THOMAS. Fine. Whatever. Now Claire, take a seat.

CLAIRE. Okay.

RYLIE. Can we help too?

CLAIRE. Help do what?

RYLIE. Make you say the "S" word.

OWEN & THOMAS. Rylie!

RYLIE. Oh, dang it. Sorry.

CLAIRE. The "S" word? What do you mean?

THOMAS. Distraction! *(He throws glitter or something in the air.)*

RYLIE. Oh, pretty!

OWEN. Thomas.

THOMAS. What?

OWEN. You can't keep dancing around the subject.

THOMAS. I don't know what you're talking about.

OWEN. Yes, you do. Now Thomas, sit. Claire, stay where you are. Rylie, go back to the box and please don't talk about you know what until it's time to.

RYLIE. Okay. *(Defeated, she goes back to the box.)*

OWEN. Alright Thomas, the floor is yours.

> *(Throughout this section* **CLAIRE** *is able to move more and more as she confesses more and more.)*

THOMAS. Alrighty, why don't you explain to me who George is?

CLAIRE. He was my best friend. We met freshman year because he was the new kid and I was the outcast so we got along pretty well.

THOMAS. Nothing strange ever happened between you two?

CLAIRE. No, everything was fine between us until now. I get that senior year is stressful with all the college applications and SATs and scholarships. I didn't expect for him to get this stressed out about it.

THOMAS. How did you know he was stressed out?

CLAIRE. He always made excuses. He always had some other thing that was more important. I know school is important, it was just hard not being able to be around him all the time, especially knowing that we'd be going our separate ways.

THOMAS. Have you talked to him about it?

CLAIRE. He never wanted to talk about it.

THOMAS. Was he happy?

CLAIRE. I thought so.

THOMAS. I need you to know.

CLAIRE. I don't know.

THOMAS. I think you do know.

> *(***CLAIRE*** *remains silent and looks at the ground.* **OWEN** *nods at him to prompt him.)*

Did he ever talk about his bad days?

CLAIRE. He was always a great listener.

THOMAS. You never asked him how he was?

CLAIRE. Of course I did! Or, at least I think I did.

THOMAS. There you go again with the "I thinks."

CLAIRE. It's been a year, give me a break!

RYLIE. A year since what?

CLAIRE. I already told you I don't want to talk about it.

THOMAS. The more you struggle the harder it is to get out.

CLAIRE. Okay, fine. I'll talk.

THOMAS. Did you know that George had depression?

OWEN. Thomas, the manual.

THOMAS. This follows the rules.

OWEN. Let *her* talk.

THOMAS. Claire, to appease Owen's request, please talk and answer my question. Did you know that George had depression?

CLAIRE. I never knew until it happened.

THOMAS. I knew.

CLAIRE. Okay, but that doesn't change the fact that he had depression, and that he never told me about it. It doesn't change the fact that I want to know why you – some guy in charge of a box – know more about my best friend than I do.

THOMAS. He doesn't want for you to worry.

CLAIRE. Well look what's happened.

THOMAS. Everything is going to be okay.

CLAIRE. How do you know this about him?

THOMAS. I already told you that I can't say.

CLAIRE. No, you tell me.

(**OWEN** *gives a nod to* **THOMAS**.)

THOMAS. Okay. I have a special talent that most other humans do not possess. I have what is known as clairempathy, which means that not only am I empathetic but also empathic, meaning I can sense what other people's emotions are without even knowing their name.

CLAIRE. That's a load of baloney.

THOMAS. Oh, but it's true! And besides, you have to trust me!

CLAIRE. Trusting and believing are two completely different things.

THOMAS. Good point. Anyway, you can't leave because of that quicksand spell I put on you.

CLAIRE. This is completely absurd. All I wanted to do was return this box and be on my merry way.

OWEN. Look, we're getting off track. Tell us about George, Claire.

RYLIE. Yeah he sounds pretty cool.

CLAIRE. He was. He was really into magic tricks. *(Smiling or even laughing at this reminiscence.)* In fact, he even had this cape and hat he would wear sometimes – it made him look like a giant dork. But he always left me baffled. He could do anything. Card tricks, doves, quick changes, you name it, he could do it.

RYLIE. That sounds oddly like someone we know. *(She glances at* **THOMAS**, *then* **OWEN** *nudges her to stop.)*

CLAIRE. He was really quirky and funny and had such a strong personality. He was always so headstrong. I guess that's why we worked so well – he was loud when I was soft-spoken, and I was personable when he was shy. I just wish he would have told me.

OWEN. Told you what?

CLAIRE. I'm not sure if I should say.

THOMAS. *(Frustrated.)* Say it Claire.

CLAIRE. I'm sorry, I just can't. **(CLAIRE** *is very defeated at this point.* **RYLIE** *and* **OWEN** *go over to console her.)*

RYLIE. Hey, it's okay.

OWEN. Yeah, this takes time.

CLAIRE. It's been a year. One whole year since it happened and all I have left of George is the lock and whatever is inside of the box and I just don't understand why I can't let this go!

THOMAS. *(He is struck with a brilliant idea.)* Well maybe I can be of some assistance to you. Owen, can you hand me the lock?

OWEN. Sure thing, boss. (**OWEN** *gives* **THOMAS** *the small box.*)

THOMAS. Thank you. Claire, may I have the key?

CLAIRE. What key?

THOMAS. I know you have it.

CLAIRE. I'm not playing hard to get, I really have no idea what you're talking about.

THOMAS. But George told me that you had the key.

CLAIRE. You talked to George?

THOMAS. Magic!

> *(He throws glitter in the air to create a diversion and jumps into the big box. The scene is frozen, and* **THOMAS** *begins talking to himself.)*

Oh, this isn't good. Claire can't know that I know him. What to do, what to do. *(He begins rummaging in the box.)* This won't do. Eh, this won't either. Maybe. Ah ha! Yes!

> *(With a snap of his fingers the scene becomes unfrozen and he ducks into the box to hide from* **CLAIRE.***)*

CLAIRE. *(She takes a moment and looks around.)* Thomas? *(Turning to* **RYLIE** *and* **OWEN.***)* Does he always do this?

OWEN. Yeah.

CLAIRE. Why?

RYLIE. He likes to avoid conflict.

OWEN. Sometimes he lets out information that only he knows and he'd prefer for it to stay that way. You see, the thing about Thomas is he cares very deeply about people like you. But sometimes it's hard for him to face the facts.

CLAIRE. What do you mean?

RYLIE. It's the "S" word.

CLAIRE. What is the "S" word?

RYLIE. I'm not allowed to say it yet.

OWEN. Only you can set yourself free.

CLAIRE. This is getting ridiculous. I'm going to be late. Thomas! Thomas I need to talk to you. *(She begins pounding the bell on his desk.)*

THOMAS. *(Popping out of the box. Sassily.)* You rang?

CLAIRE. I'm not angry with you that you talked to George.

THOMAS. Who said I talked to George?

CLAIRE. You did.

OWEN. The girl ain't lyin'.

RYLIE. Thomas, why don't you just tell her.

CLAIRE. Tell me what?

THOMAS. Claire, why don't you sit down.

CLAIRE. So I take it that this is bad news.

THOMAS. It all depends on how you look at it.

CLAIRE. Just say it.

THOMAS. But first –

CLAIRE. Ugh!

THOMAS. Why don't you take a look into this. *(THOMAS hands her what resembles a snow globe. It is a jar full of glitter and water and anything that sparkles.)*

CLAIRE. A snow globe?

OWEN. It looks like a jar.

RYLIE. Oh my gosh, glitter!

THOMAS. It's much more than that. Come on, come on, start staring into "The Mystical Sphere of Wonders."

CLAIRE. That's an odd thing to call a snow globe.

THOMAS. It's not a snow globe, it's "The Mystical Sphere of Wonders"!

CLAIRE. What am I supposed to be looking for?

THOMAS. The key to your happiness, quite literally.

CLAIRE. I just see glitter. And rhinestones.

THOMAS. That's the wonder. Maybe if you just hold it up to the light.

> *(He takes her hands and puts the globe higher in the air.)*

CLAIRE. I think I see something!

THOMAS. What does it look like?

CLAIRE. A key, obviously.

THOMAS. Good, good. Now, you see why I wanted you to gaze into the sphere. That's what George saw too.

CLAIRE. Really?

THOMAS. Yes.

CLAIRE. Well that makes me happy.

THOMAS. I told him it would.

CLAIRE. Thank you.

THOMAS. It's my pleasure.

> *(**THOMAS** and **CLAIRE** have this weird moment of understanding. **OWEN** and **RYLIE** look at each other, completely lost as to what is going on.)*

OWEN. So for the people over here that don't have clairvanity or whatever, we'd like to know why this makes you so happy.

RYLIE. Yeah, I'm totally lost.

CLAIRE. Guys, I just don't feel comfortable talking about it.

THOMAS. Why not?

CLAIRE. This just isn't something you talk about.

THOMAS. What?

CLAIRE. Thomas, you know.

THOMAS. Quicksand.

CLAIRE. Don't start that crap again.

THOMAS. Why? Does it make you mad?

CLAIRE. Yes.

THOMAS. Does it make you crazy?

CLAIRE. Yes!

THOMAS. Come on Owen, Rylie. Say it with me: Quicksand.

OWEN. Quicksand.

RYLIE. Quicksand.

> *(**THOMAS**, **OWEN**, and **RYLIE** keep chanting "Quicksand" together until **CLAIRE** breaks through.)*

CLAIRE. Suicide! Suicide. George committed suicide. Are you happy now? Because I'm not. Because all he left me was this stupid lock that I don't have the key to and now I'm left in silence because I miss him so much. I don't want to talk about it because of how much it hurts. Okay? Is that what you all wanted to hear?

THOMAS. Congratulations, Claire.

RYLIE. You said the "S" word.

OWEN. You have just completed step two. (*He holds up a sign that says "Step Two: Complete."*)

CLAIRE. What next?

THOMAS. We talk about it.

CLAIRE. I'm tired of answering so many questions.

THOMAS. How else are you going to get out of the quicksand?

CLAIRE. Stop asking so many questions and answer some yourself.

THOMAS. Okay. What would you like to know?

CLAIRE. How did you end up here?

THOMAS. Easy. Because no one wants to talk about it.

CLAIRE. Talk about what?

THOMAS. The "S" word.

CLAIRE. After all that you put me through, even you won't say it?

THOMAS. Nope.

CLAIRE. And why is that.

THOMAS. I'm taking a vow of silence.

CLAIRE. You can't do that!

> (**THOMAS** *hands her the manual and points to a section for her to read.*)

(*Reading out of manual.*) "I can do whatever I want, I'm in charge and you aren't. Hahaha."

> (**THOMAS** *smugly shakes his head.*)

Okay, fair enough.

THOMAS. Enough of that. I like the sound of my voice too much to not talk. Now Claire, would you like to know why I took a vow of silence?

CLAIRE. Sure.

THOMAS. It's because people don't talk about it. Most everyone chooses to stay silent, whether it's the person who needs help or the family and friends of the victims. It's death, it's murder – but of yourself, and no one wants to talk about it so it just keeps happening!

RYLIE. Thomas, it's okay.

THOMAS. No, it's not okay. You should know that. You should be just as mad as I am that no one will talk about it.

CLAIRE. I didn't mean to make you mad.

THOMAS. This is more than just about you, Claire. It's about the people who are left to wonder where they went wrong and why the people they were so close to just decided that one day life wasn't worth living anymore. You have no idea how many lost people come through here day in and day out. You have no idea what it's like to feel so miserable for them because whatever they are feeling, I feel too. And I never thought that I could experience a pain any harsher than my own, but I have. And it's in you Claire.

CLAIRE. How is that even possible?

THOMAS. Because I knew George. I saw with my own two eyes the center of your happiness. I know what his voice sounds like, what kind of clothes he wears. I know that he loved magic. I know how much he loved you because you were one of the only good people in his life who accepted him as he was. I know him and now I know you. And you were the one person who could have stopped it.

CLAIRE. You are *not* putting the blame on me.

RYLIE. You know that's not true.

THOMAS. I'm sorry. Claire –

CLAIRE. No. I already feel bad enough without Mr. Box Dude telling me that I could have prevented my best friend's death. Can you tell me how I could have stopped him? Because if he was this unhappy for so long and I didn't know it then how would you?

THOMAS. I have my ways.

CLAIRE. I cannot believe you right now!

THOMAS. Why not?

CLAIRE. You should know, Mr. Empathic.

THOMAS. And for once, I don't. I don't know how you could have stopped George from killing himself. You couldn't even if you tried. I don't know why my aunt decided to do it. I don't know why Rylie's boyfriend did it or why Owen's brother did the same. But what I do know is that we are all suffering together in silence and it shouldn't be this way.

CLAIRE. Rylie, is that true?

> (**RYLIE** *nods "yes."*)

And Owen?

OWEN. The very same.

CLAIRE. I'm so sorry.

RYLIE. It's okay.

OWEN. It's not your fault.

CLAIRE. I think that I'm ready to talk now.

THOMAS. Good. So why was this box so important to the both of you?

CLAIRE. Towards the end of freshman year George thought he might move towns again, so I gave him this lock. He told me that he never had a friend like me, that I was something special, and that no matter what happened to us I'd always be locked up in his heart. Like I was some sort of prisoner. Well, I kind of am now, I guess. He's the one locked up in my mind and I just can't get him out of my head and it's all just too much sometimes. I miss him so much, you can't even imagine.

RYLIE. Where is the key he's talking about?

CLAIRE. He never told me about it. He never told me a lot of things.

RYLIE. Why do you think he did it?

CLAIRE. To escape something, I guess. He always talked about wanting to get away from it all, I didn't know that he meant life. You know, sometimes he did look sad but happiness is a choice, I always just thought that he chose not to be happy.

RYLIE. Happiness is a choice, but for depressed people it's not an option.

OWEN. If George could have chosen to be happy, don't you think he would have?

CLAIRE. Of course.

OWEN. And Claire, aren't you here because you're unhappy?

CLAIRE. I guess so.

OWEN. So why not just choose to be happy?

RYLIE. You see, mental illness isn't that easy.

OWEN. It's hard to understand these things unless you've gone through them yourself.

CLAIRE. I just wish that I had known that he wanted it all to end. I wish that I could have stopped it. I didn't know he wanted to die.

OWEN. None of us did.

CLAIRE. But how can I be happy now when he's gone?

THOMAS. Don't you get it? He doesn't want you to be upset about this.

RYLIE. No one who's committed suicide ever does.

OWEN. It all goes back to how they were feeling.

THOMAS. Sad.

RYLIE. Mad.

OWEN. Alone.

THOMAS. And all these things that the people we love have been feeling for so long make them feel like they are making us sad, too.

RYLIE. And their raincloud suddenly turns into a thunderstorm.

OWEN. It's selfish.

THOMAS. It's upsetting.

RYLIE. It's horrible.

OWEN. It's brutal.

THOMAS. They honestly think that this world is better off without them.

RYLIE. That no one will notice that they are gone.

OWEN. That they leave without a trace.

THOMAS. But they are wrong.

RYLIE. I miss Jack every day.

OWEN. Steve never got to see me graduate.

THOMAS. My aunt never got to see who I became.

RYLIE. There was a deafening silence surrounding his death.

OWEN. Everyone had questions.

THOMAS. But no one had answers.

OWEN. No one wanted to talk about it.

THOMAS. But I knew that everyone did.

RYLIE. But you can be different, Claire.

OWEN. Don't make the same mistakes that we did.

THOMAS. And now do you see why we want to help you?

RYLIE. Because you can be different, Claire.

OWEN. Don't get stuck in the quicksand.

THOMAS. Claire, what's today's date?

CLAIRE. April 18, 2016. [**Or the actual date.**]

THOMAS. And why is today significant?

CLAIRE. Because a year ago today I lost my best friend.

THOMAS. Claire, where are you going?

CLAIRE. I'm going to a memorial.

THOMAS. Whose?

CLAIRE. George's.

RYLIE. It's going to get better, Claire. You know, Jack left a hole in my life so big that I have to wait around in a lost and found box all day, just waiting to try and make someone else smile because I couldn't make myself smile. You never realize just how important someone is until they're gone. He just left. He just decided that he was done and no one could stop him. How is that fair? And when I was going through his possessions after he died, I found a ring. *(She shows* **CLAIRE** *the ring on her finger.)* I never knew why he didn't propose to me, and after that I just had to leave our apartment. So I came across this place and Owen took me in. So now I live here in the Lost and Found, and after all this time, I've discovered something: Jack wouldn't want for me to be sad. He would want me to be a light to others, and so I stay here, not because I'm still sad, but because I need to help people like you, for Jack.

OWEN. Steve never realized just how much I needed him to guide me. He didn't think of his baby brother or his mom or anyone else. And I'm the selfish one for not wanting him to go. I kept praying to God, *(He holds up his Bible.)* waiting to find my answers. I wasn't supposed to hold on to hate. I'm not supposed to be mad at Steve. I'm supposed to love my big brother with all my heart. Because at the end of the day tragedies are just that, but there has always been a bigger plan for me, up in the sky. And Steve would be happy to know that I'm helping people like you.

THOMAS. My aunt never realized how proud she would be one day to see me helping people like you. But I guess that things happen for a reason. Because if she never died I would have never met you, Claire. I would have never gotten to unlock your happiness. Claire, what's that chain around your neck?

CLAIRE. What chain? *(She discovers she's wearing a necklace with a key pendant.)* What? What is this?

OWEN. It looks like a key.

CLAIRE. How did this get here? This is like a magic trick that George would do.

THOMAS. Claire, it was there the whole time. You just weren't looking hard enough.

OWEN. Sometimes the things that we need the most are right under our noses.

RYLIE. Let's unlock this thing!

(**RYLIE** *turns the key and the lock opens. She proceeds to open the small box. It's empty.*)

CLAIRE. Nothing. There's nothing in here. Thomas, I don't understand – how is this supposed to help?

THOMAS. All those years ago in Mrs. Byboth's literature class, George realized one thing: he wanted to make at least someone happy, even if it couldn't be himself. And that person is you, Claire. George has given you the key to your happiness.

CLAIRE. Wait, I never said anything about Mrs. Byboth. George? George, is that you?

(**THOMAS** *has transformed. He wears a wizard's cloak.*)

GEORGE. Hey there, loser!

CLAIRE. George! *(They embrace for a long time.)* I've missed you.

GEORGE. I've missed you too, Claire.

CLAIRE. I'm so sorry.

GEORGE. Sorry? For what?

CLAIRE. I'm your best friend, I should have known.

GEORGE. Claire –

CLAIRE. No, no, I'm sorry. I just, I miss you so much, I want you back, I need you George.

GEORGE. Claire – have you not heard a word of anything I told you?

CLAIRE. Psh, no! Like I'd listen to some dork who does magic tricks.

GEORGE. Oh, come on, those are cool. And how about that quicksand trick huh? Huh? *(He gently nudges her.)*

CLAIRE. Yeah, that was awesome! But how did you end up here?

GEORGE. The Lost and Found is a magical place where people come to find the things that they lost. Sometimes it's as simple as a jacket or a wallet. Sometimes it's a part of yourself. I needed the closure just as much as you, Claire. I needed to know that you got the key and that you were okay. I left my box on your front step a year ago in my last attempt at a suicide note, but I could never bring myself to write one. But you knew, Claire. You knew me better than anyone. And now, I'm the one who has to apologize, because I'm sorry that I've put you through all of this. But in my defense, I thought you'd come a lot sooner. Man, you were always so dramatic.

CLAIRE. Was not!

GEORGE. Was so!

CLAIRE. That was a pretty clever trick you pulled.

GEORGE. Well, I can't take all the credit, I had two very brilliant assistants.

CLAIRE. Rylie, Owen, you guys knew?

OWEN. Yeah.

RYLIE. Of course! George is great.

OWEN. In fact, I'm actually the boss of the Lost and Found. You never saw this place because you were always in denial that it actually existed. George has been here for a whole year.

RYLIE. We've been waiting for you for a very long time.

OWEN. Well Claire, congratulations!

RYLIE. You have just completed step three! *(She holds up a sign that says "Step Three: Complete.")*

CLAIRE. And what's that?

RYLIE. Acceptance.

CLAIRE. Thank you two so much, it's been a pleasure meeting you.

RYLIE. Any time.

OWEN. Well Claire, I believe you're running late to a very important memorial for a very special friend. *(He nudges* **GEORGE,** *or gives him a look.)*

CLAIRE. Thank you. *(They all hug.)*

OWEN. I can see that little glimmer of hope in your eyes. Don't lose it, Claire.

RYLIE. You have found something that none of us have found yet.

CLAIRE. Hope?

RYLIE. And a lock.

OWEN. And a key.

GEORGE. And your happiness. And now that you've come, my job here is done.

CLAIRE. What? No. You just got here, you can't leave again.

GEORGE. Claire, I've been here the whole time – the lock, the box, the key, all of it. I gave you the key to wear around your neck because I'll always be close to your heart. I gave you the lock because I'll always be holding your hand. And the box: to leave you wondering, so that I'm always on your mind.

RYLIE. Just because he's dead doesn't mean that he's gone.

OWEN. *(Consulting the manual.)* George, I'm afraid it's time to say goodbye.

GEORGE. *(He gives the box and lock back to* **CLAIRE.** *He snaps his fingers.)* The quicksand spell is now gone. You are free.

CLAIRE. I love you, George.

GEORGE. I love you too, Claire.

(They hug.)

CLAIRE. I'll never forget you, George. You'll always be close to my heart.

GEORGE. Claire, just one more thing before I leave.

CLAIRE. Yes?

> (**GEORGE** *pulls her away from the big box.* **OWEN** *and* **RYLIE** *both go back into it.* **GEORGE** *and* **CLAIRE** *kneel at center, and* **GEORGE** *puts the small box in front of them. He holds the little padlock, and* **CLAIRE** *holds the key.*)

GEORGE. Our happiness is not based on a person. Only you can truly find what you've lost. You will always be my best friend, and I will always care about you. I'm still with you, even if I'm gone. Just look at that key when you miss me. It will solve so many of your problems.

CLAIRE. Goodbye, George. (*She puts the key into the box.*)

GEORGE. Goodbye, Claire. (*He puts the lock in the box and closes it.*)

End of Play

Casey Durso as Claire (center) surrounded by the quirky characters played by Paul Fico, Elizabeth Miller, and Jonathan Connolly in the Thespian Festival staged reading of *Lost and Found*, by Alyssa Faykus.

The Third Wall

Kim Wong

The Third Wall, by Kim Wong of Troupe 2661 at Wichita (Kansas) Northwest High School, was presented in a staged reading as part of the Thespian Playworks program at the 2016 Thespian Festival on June 24. William Myatt was director, Lindsay Price served as dramaturg, and Kyle Nohea Awai served as stage manager. The cast was as follows:

PENELOPE #1 . . . . Kayla Temshiv

PENELOPE #2 . . . . .Deirdre Price

ANNA #1 . . . . Erin Hyatt

ANNA # 2 . . . . Emily Rux

STEVEN . . . . Kevin Lacey

CHARACTERS

PENELOPE #1 – An educated rising playwright stuck in a drab day job. Dressed like Penelope #2, in office attire. Driven by curiosity. Has writer's block.

ANNA #1 – Penelope #1's longtime friend. Ditsy and somewhat conceited.

PENELOPE #2 – Same as Penelope #1, but driven by her desire to have control. Her personality comes to life as Penelope #1 and Anna #1 write about her.

ANNA #2 – Same as Anna #1, but more exaggerated and over-dramatic, a real ham. Also brought into existence by Penelope #1 and Anna #1.

SOFIA – A character created by Penelope #1 and Penelope #2 – so she knows only what is written by them.

AUTHOR'S NOTES

Sofia and the two Annas may be recast as male roles, using the names Steven and Alan. Pronouns are key words in the script. Pay close attention to the stage directions as well as the script that is being written as the play unfolds: this reveals much about the characters coming to life.

(A wall is center stage, dividing two identical sets: on each side of the wall stands a desk equipped with a laptop and an office chair. Upstage right and left, a door. **PENELOPE #2** *is concealed behind the desk stage left.* **PENELOPE #1** *is sitting behind the desk stage right. Lighting may be used to punctuate the action shifts from one side of the stage to the other – in which case, lights up stage right.)*

PENELOPE #1. I had an idea...but...I can't seem to remember it... This is some serious *déjà vu...* Hmmm...

(Inspiration hits. The next lines are said as though reading stage directions. **PENELOPE #1** *starts typing. Lights dim stage right.)*

A desk and chair stage left. A wall center stage.

(Lights up stage left.)

A writer is at the desk, concentrating.

*(***PENELOPE #2*** rises and sits at the desk.)*

PENELOPE #2. *(Thinking. Sounding clichéd.)* What to write, what to write... Hmmm... How about? *(Beat.)* No... What if? *(Beat.)* No...

(Lights up stage right. Stage left lights dim. **PENELOPE #2** *freezes.)*

PENELOPE #1. I can't start a show like that. She doesn't sound...real.

*(***PENELOPE #1*** backspaces on the laptop. Sits and thinks, then starts typing again. Lights up stage left. Stage right lights down.)*

PENELOPE #2. *(Grandiose.)* My show will revolutionize the playwriting industry. It'll win a Pulitzer Prize. I'll finally be recognized for all the long hours I put into this stinkin' show. *(Beat.)* The only problem is coming up with another good idea... I can't do it. I can't meet this stupid deadline...

(Lights up stage right. Stage left lights down.)

PENELOPE #1. Wait, this isn't my diary! People would fall asleep if the show was about me. *(A dejected beat.)* That's it! I can't do this anymore. Everyone is going to forget who I am... I'm going to fail.

*(Knock at door stage right. **PENELOPE #1** is startled. **ANNA #1** enters.)*

ANNA #1. Hey, Penelope. I thought maybe I'd take you out to lunch today.

PENELOPE #1. Later, Anna. I've got to work on this.

ANNA #1. Whoa. No need to be so snippy.

PENELOPE #1. Sorry, I'm under a lot of stress.

ANNA #1. Why?

PENELOPE #1. It's the deal.

ANNA #1. What deal?

PENELOPE #1. But's it's not a big one.

ANNA #1. What do you mean? You're acting strange...

PENELOPE #1. The contract. It's not a big deal.

ANNA #1. What contract? You haven't told me about this.

PENELOPE #1. Like I said, it's not a big deal.

ANNA #1. *What's* not a big deal?! What's going on?

PENELOPE #1. A director from New York offered me a contract paying a lot of money and it's not a big deal.

ANNA #1. Penelope! That *is* a big deal! *(Beat.)* Why didn't you tell me sooner? We could've gone out and celebrated.

PENELOPE #1. I didn't think you would care that much.

ANNA #1. What?! Of course I would care.

PENELOPE #1. You've seen how my other shows are a big hit, *here*. This shouldn't surprise you. This isn't any different... At least, that's what I'm trying to make myself believe...

ANNA #1. You've done it before, right? Why can't you do it again?

PENELOPE #1. It's this stupid deadline. All the other times I've written a play, I wasn't under much pressure but now...

ANNA #1. What happens if you don't meet this deadline?

PENELOPE #1. I don't even want to think about that.

ANNA #1. *(Beat.)* You're writing during work again? Aren't you going to get behind?

PENELOPE #1. If my boss finds out I'm doing this, I'll probably get fired.

ANNA #1. Penelope...

PENELOPE #1. And I've never even met him – or her. We only communicate through email so if anyone comes in, I have to look busy.

ANNA #1. Is that why you jumped in your seat when I came in?

PENELOPE #1. Yeah. *(Laughs.)* I was scared for a moment. But maybe, *maybe,* my job won't matter... If I become a successful playwright and move to New York, I'd be living the dream. But until then, this two-dimensional office work will have to do.

ANNA #1. Are you at least making progress in your writing?

PENELOPE #1. No.

ANNA #1. Why do you say that?

PENELOPE #1. Because I can't. I can't write any more. I can't think of another great idea. And I can't let my director down.

ANNA #1. At least you *can* sit there and write a whole show. I don't think I could ever do that.

PENELOPE #1. What do you mean, "sit there and write a show"? You stand in front of hundreds of people and recite lines without messing up.

ANNA #1. I don't just recite all those lines, I act. I put my own twist on the characters I play, I bring to life what is written on the page. And the feeling onstage is...

amazing. *(Becoming self-absorbed.)* Everyone looking up at you, cheering, throwing flowers at you, blowing kisses –

PENELOPE #1. Anna!

ANNA #1. Oh, sorry. It's just that sitting at a desk is so boring.

PENELOPE #1. It's not boring!

ANNA #1. Oh, really?

PENELOPE #1. I find it more entertaining to watch my ideas, the words that I wrote on a piece of paper, come to life as my show is produced. Then, I get to kick back and enjoy the show from the audience point of view.

ANNA #1. Pfft. *(Under her breath.)* With nobody paying attention to you? … *(Normal voice level.)* What kind of show were you thinking of this time?

PENELOPE #1. I'm going for a comedy.

ANNA #1. Why don't you…write about your life?

PENELOPE #1. Are you saying my life is a joke?

ANNA #1. Well…

PENELOPE #1. Ha ha. That's so original. Anyways, what little writing I *did* get done does sound a little like my life right now.

ANNA #1. Let me see.

(**ANNA #1** *leans over to read computer screen.*)

Why does it say "by Pen Kuh-name"?

PENELOPE #1. The K is silent.

ANNA #1. Ohhh… Pen "Name."

PENELOPE #1. It's my pen name. Pen is short for Penelope. And I spelled "name" with a K because it's clever.

ANNA #1. Okay. Very clever. *(Pause. Continues reading.)* Yup. It does sound like you right now. I have an idea. Since you already started writing about your life, you can't have it without me.

(*She sits next to* **PENELOPE #1** *and begins typing. Lights come up stage left. Stage right lights go dim.*)

ANNA #2. Hey, girl! Whatcha workin' on?

PENELOPE #2. I'm trying to write an award-winning, rear-jerking –

> *(Spotlight on desk, stage right.* **PENELOPE #2** *and* **ANNA #2** *freeze.)*

PENELOPE #1. *(Laughing.)* Rear-jerking?

ANNA #1. I meant to say *tear*-jerking.

> *(She backspaces. Spotlight goes down stage right.* **PENELOPE #2** *and* **ANNA #2** *resume.)*

PENELOPE #2. – Tear-jerking, jaw-dropping show, but I'm having no luck.

ANNA #2. Why don't you ask the audience for help?

> *(She turns to the audience. Lights come up stage right; stage left lights go down.* **PENELOPE #2** *and* **ANNA #2** *freeze.)*

PENELOPE #1. Anna! Don't write that. I think it's a low form of comedy when the writer has to turn to breaking the fourth wall.

ANNA #1. It's not that bad. Plus it's always a lot of fun. You never know how the audience is going to react.

PENELOPE #1. Exactly! Which is why it's so risky. They might just sit there and not do anything or say something really bad or not play along…

ANNA #1. C'mon, Penelope. Just this once. I'm helping you out, okay?

PENELOPE #1. I'll take it from here.

> *(She starts typing again. Lights come up stage left. Stage right is dimly lit.)*

PENELOPE #2. What audience? All I see is a wall.

ANNA #2. Fine. I guess breaking the fourth wall isn't a good idea. These walls are pretty thick and I'll end up conkin' my noggin.

PENELOPE #2. Yeah. But for you it probably wouldn't hurt that much since you're so thick-headed.

> *(Lights come up stage right. Stage left is dimly lit.)*

ANNA #1. Hey! I'm not thick-headed.

> *(She starts typing again. Lights come up stage left. Stage right is dimly lit.)*

ANNA #2. How about, instead of breaking the fourth wall, we break the third wall?

> *(Lights come up stage right. Next two lines are spoken by both doppelgangers simultaneously.)*

PENELOPE #1 & #2. What is that even supposed to mean?

ANNA #1 & #2. You'll see.

> **(PENELOPE #2** *dismisses* **ANNA #2** *and concentrates on the computer.* **ANNA #2** *breaks through the wall center stage.* **PENELOPE #1** *and* **ANNA #1** *scream. All but* **PENELOPE #2** *are stunned.)*

PENELOPE #2. What's all that screaming about?

ANNA #2. Uhhh…

PENELOPE #1. How did you do that?

ANNA #1. I didn't do anything!

PENELOPE #1. There isn't supposed to be anything on the other side of the wall. It leads outside!

ANNA #1. I know!

> **(PENELOPE #1** *and* **ANNA #1** *stare at* **ANNA #2**.*)*

PENELOPE #1. She kind of looks like you. *(Beat.)* She's also dressed like you.

ANNA #1. Who are you?

ANNA #2. I'm Anna.

ANNA #1. Anna? That's my name.

PENELOPE #2. *(Nonchalant.)* Who are you talking to? And where did you go?

ANNA #2. I think I'm lost.

PENELOPE #2. *(Finally looks away from her screen, leaning over desk.)* Is that another office? There shouldn't be anything on the other side of the wall. It leads outside.

ANNA #2. It's supposed to…

(PENELOPE #2 *starts to cross stage right.*)

PENELOPE #1. I let you help me write a show and you end up destroying my office?!

ANNA #1. I didn't mean to –

PENELOPE #2. What do you mean, your office? There shouldn't be anything on the other side of *my* wall. *(To* **ANNA #2.***)* What were you thinking? "Breaking the third wall." You're an idiot!

ANNA #1 & #2. (**ANNA #1** *speaks defensively;* **ANNA #2** *speaks apologetically.*) I didn't mean to break anything.

PENELOPE #2. And why are they dressed like us?!

ANNA #2. I don't know.

PENELOPE #1. Where did you two come from? *(Turns to* **ANNA #1.***)* This is your fault! You brought them here. You started writing on my computer, "Anna breaks the third wall." And now, these freaky people are here with no explanation. *(Sighs exasperatedly.)* This doesn't make sense… They shouldn't even exist. There is nothing on the other side of that wall!

ANNA #2. We shouldn't exist? What is that supposed to mean? How do we know you're not supposed to "exist"?

PENELOPE #2. Wait, you were writing on your computer?

ANNA #1. Yes. We both were.

PENELOPE #2. May I see what you wrote?

PENELOPE #1. Go ahead.

(**PENELOPE #2** *crosses to computer and reads the screen.*)

PENELOPE #2. This is the same conversation we had earlier.

ANNA #2. What? *(She crosses to computer, reads the screen.)* It is…

PENELOPE #2. How is that possible?

ANNA #1. Do you think maybe, when we started writing this, we created an alternate, parallel-universe, *Star Trek*-y thing that brought them into our world?

PENELOPE #1. That's ridiculous!

ANNA #2. What other explanation could there be? Oh no! Does that mean we're not supposed to exist, since they started writing our conversation? *(Melodramatic.)* Is our whole life a lie?

PENELOPE #2. No, that's impossible.

PENELOPE #1. It sounds impossible, but I think you may be right, Anna… *(Pondering.)* Controlling someone's fate by writing –

PENELOPE #2. You control us? I don't think so! How do I know that you didn't spy on us, write down our conversation, and pull some sort of stupid prank on us?

ANNA #1. How would a prank like that even work?

ANNA #2. The other Anna is right. There can't be another explanation.

PENELOPE #1. *(To* ANNA #1 *and* ANNA #2.*)* Oh, stop it!

ANNA #1. If you started typing on your computer again, would you be controlling them?

PENELOPE #1. I don't know, and I don't want to try it out.

ANNA #2. Can we just fix this wall and pretend this never happened?

PENELOPE #1. I don't think it's going to be that easy.

PENELOPE #2. Whatever you do, you and your friend need to go back to not existing so things go back to normal.

PENELOPE #1. We need to stop existing?! I'm the one that wrote you –

PENELOPE #2. You don't know that for sure –

PENELOPE #1. But I –

ANNA #1. Hey other Anna! Let's go outside to see if the building is broken!

ANNA #2. That sounds like a great idea! I'll go this way, *(Indicates stage right.)* and you go that way. *(Indicates stage left.)*

       (ANNA #1 *exits stage left.* ANNA #2 *exits stage right.)*

PENELOPE #1. Hurry back soon!

PENELOPE #2. *(Sincerely.)* Don't get lost! *(To* **PENELOPE #1.***)* You know Anna can be so scatterbrained sometimes. *(Beat.)* What would happen if we just wrote a new character? What would that make them?

PENELOPE #1. I'm not sure. I really don't feel comfortable writing anything else until we figure this out.

PENELOPE #2. Okay, then I'll do it. *(Crosses to computer and begins typing.)* A new character, Sofia, enters stage left.

> *(As* **PENELOPE #2** *is narrating,* **SOFIA** *enters stage left.)*

SOFIA. Are you the one making all this noise? Penelope, what happened to your office?!

> *(***PENELOPE #2** *panics. As she is backspacing,* **SOFIA** *walks backwards and exits the way she came.)*

PENELOPE #1. Why did you do that? Did you just erase her out of existence?

PENELOPE #2. *(Nonchalant.)* Who knows? I've never seen her before.

PENELOPE #1. Wait, did you control what she said or did she control what you typed?

PENELOPE #2. I don't know. I can't really tell.

PENELOPE #1. Bring her back! We can't just write someone to life and kill her off.

PENELOPE #2. Fine. I'll bring her back. *(Begins typing.)* A new character, Sofia, enters stage left.

> *(As* **PENELOPE #2** *is narrating,* **SOFIA** *enters stage left.)*

SOFIA. Are you the one making all this noise? Penelope, what happened to your office?! Is this some sick prank? Penelope, you're fired!!

PENELOPE #2. No, I'm not. *(Backspaces a few times.* **SOFIA** *again backs out toward exit.)*

PENELOPE #1. Stop doing that!

> *(***SOFIA** *freezes in front of door.)*

PENELOPE #2. We can't lose our job, she was about to fire us! *(Continues to backspace.)*

*(****SOFIA**** exits stage left.)*

PENELOPE #1. Stop! Don't backspace that far!

*(****PENELOPE #2**** continues to backspace. Then **PENELOPE #1** and **PENELOPE #2** are in a trance for a moment; they have forgotten the character they just wrote.)*

PENELOPE #2. You know Anna can be so scatterbrained sometimes. *(Beat.)* What would happen if we just wrote a new character? What would that make them?

PENELOPE #1. I'm not sure. I really don't feel comfortable writing anything else until we figure this out.

PENELOPE #2. Okay, then I'll do it. *(Begins typing.)* A new character, Sofia, enters stage left.

*(As ****PENELOPE #2**** is narrating, **SOFIA** enters stage left.)*

SOFIA. Are you the one making all this noise? Penelope, what happened to your office?!

*(****PENELOPE #2**** panics. As she is backspacing, **SOFIA** yet again walks backwards and exits.)*

PENELOPE #1. Why did you do that? Did you just erase her out of existence?

PENELOPE #2. *(Nonchalant.)* Who knows? I've never seen her before.

PENELOPE #1. Wait, did you control what she said or did she control what you typed?

PENELOPE #2. I don't know. I can't really tell.

PENELOPE #1. Bring her back! We can't just write someone to life and kill her off.

PENELOPE #2. Fine. I'll bring her back. *(Begins typing.)* A new character, Sofia, enters stage left.

*(As ****PENELOPE #2**** is narrating, **SOFIA** enters stage left.)*

SOFIA. Are you the one making all this noise? Penelope, what happened to your office?! Is this some sick prank? Penelope, you're fired!!

PENELOPE #2. No I'm not.

> *(She backspaces a few times.* **SOFIA** *yet again walks backwards toward exit.)*

PENELOPE #1. Stop doing that!

> *(As* **PENELOPE #2** *stops backspacing,* **SOFIA** *stops moving.)*

PENELOPE #2. We can't lose our job, she was about to fire us!

> *(She continues to backspace.* **SOFIA** *continues walking backwards toward exit.)*

PENELOPE #1. Stop! Don't backspace that far!

> *(***PENELOPE #1** *stops* **PENELOPE #2** *from backspacing any more.* **SOFIA** *stops walking.)*

You were about to erase the scene where Anna breaks the third wall, and we don't know what will happen if you're erased.

PENELOPE #2. *(Beat.)* You're right.

PENELOPE #1. *(Beat.)* It's not fair that you would obliterate Sofia if I didn't stop you. How would you feel if I erased you and your Anna out of existence?

PENELOPE #2. I honestly wouldn't know. If we never existed, we would never remember having thoughts, feelings, or experiences. You know, sometimes I wonder, what if we are all just part of some show, or a person's imagination, with our fate in someone else's hand, and we have no control over what we do. Everything is thought out, predetermined, pre-programed, pre-planned, and no matter what we do, the outcome is always the same. But we wouldn't even know because we don't have a mind of our own.

PENELOPE #1. Don't say that. The difference between reality and fiction is the ability to make our own choices. Making decisions, being different, having free will is what makes us real, makes us alive. To disagree would be like admitting that you're not real.

PENELOPE #2. I don't have time to argue about philosophy right now. My job is on the line and she needs to go.

(PENELOPE #2 starts to backspace. SOFIA backs up to door. Then, PENELOPE #1 shuts down the computer. SOFIA freezes in front of door. PENELOPE #2 gasps and checks to see if she is still there.)

You could have killed me!

PENELOPE #1. Maybe – but we still haven't figured out exactly what is going on.

PENELOPE #2. So? You can't just… *(Looks at SOFIA.)* erase me…

(ANNA #1 enters stage left. ANNA #2 enters stage right.)

ANNA #1. I didn't see any broken walls on the outside of the building.

ANNA #2. Neither did I. Everything looked A-OK. *(Indicating SOFIA.)* Who is she?

PENELOPE #1. Her name is Sofia. We wrote her.

(Pause. All look at SOFIA.)

ANNA #1. Can she talk?

SOFIA. Yeah?

(All are startled.)

PENELOPE #1. How do you feel?

SOFIA. Fine, I guess. My head is a bit foggy.

PENELOPE #1. Where did you come from?

SOFIA. The hallway?

PENELOPE #1. No, I meant –

SOFIA. And why are there two Penelopes and two Annas?

PENELOPE #2. We're trying to figure that out right now.

SOFIA. I'm so confused. My head is spinning in circles.

ANNA #2. How did you know our names?

SOFIA. I just...know. Penelope is my accountant, and you, Anna, visit Penelope at work a lot.

PENELOPE #1. Can you tell us anything you remember before walking through that door?

SOFIA. I remember hearing a lot of noise...

PENELOPE #1. Besides that, anything beforehand?

SOFIA. No...

PENELOPE #1. *(Beat.)* Do you know what you had for breakfast this morning?

SOFIA. No...

PENELOPE #2. What gave you the authority to fire us?

SOFIA. I own this business.

PENELOPE #2. What exactly is this business?

SOFIA. It's...a...

PENELOPE #2. Where do you live?

SOFIA. I don't know –

PENELOPE #2. How old are you?

SOFIA. I, I don't –

PENELOPE #2. When is your birthday?

SOFIA. I – ohhh, my head...

PENELOPE #1. Stop it! Give her a break.

PENELOPE #2. *(Pause.)* What did you say before you were about to leave the room?

SOFIA. What do you mean? I just got here. I wasn't about to leave the room and I haven't said anything since you wondered if I could talk.

PENELOPE #2. You mean, you don't remember firing me?

SOFIA. No.

PENELOPE #2. *(To* **PENELOPE #1,** *quietly.)* Did you hear that? She doesn't remember firing us because I backspaced what she said. I think I controlled her. She doesn't have a mind of her own.

PENELOPE #1. *(Quietly.)* Look at her. She has to have a mind of her own. The computer is turned off but she's still here. You're still here. Your Anna is still here.

(ANNA #1 *walks to* PENELOPE #1 *and* PENELOPE
#2. ANNA #2 *follows.*)

ANNA #1. *(Quietly.)* Okay, what is going on?

PENELOPE #2. Nothing.

ANNA #1. You can't say "nothing" is going on!

PENELOPE #1. That Penelope is trying to say that we don't have free will but I say we do.

ANNA #2. *(Pondering; to herself.)* My own free will… *(At a normal voice level.)* So, what you're saying is: I could just…just… Man! I forgot it.

ANNA #1. Your lines?

ANNA #2. Yeah. That would give me a reason to go off-script and ad lib. Something like… *(She utters something spontaneous and random, such as "I love chocolate!" "There is no intelligent life on this planet; beam me up, Scotty!" references to earlier productions, current events, etc.)* Then, I could jump out into the audience – *(She suddenly jumps offstage.)*

PENELOPE #2. Where'd she go?

ANNA #2. …And ask them something like, "Excuse me, do you know where I am? *(Pause or interrupt if audience member responds.)* Oh, never mind. I can see the stage is just right there. *(Looks at her wrist with no watch.)* Oh, my! That late already. It's past my bedtime. *(Yawns really big.)* Just kidding! *(Watches characters onstage.)* I guess I better quit stalling and get back to the show." *(Climbs onstage.)* Just like that?

PENELOPE #2. Where did you come from? I lost you after you said "jump into the audience."

ANNA #2. *(Continues; ignoring her.)* Which would prove the other Penelope's point. We do have free will because I decided to leave and talk to the audience.

ANNA #1. An audience?! Was it a full house?

ANNA #2. There was about –

PENELOPE #1. Anna, other Anna, stop fooling around!

PENELOPE #2. But like I said, what if we are part of a show and the script says to do whatever you just did?

ANNA #2. If you find a script that has our entire life written out, then show me and we'll agree with you that we don't have free will.

> *(A script is thrown from offstage at actors onstage.* **SOFIA** *picks it up.)*

SOFIA. What's this? … "*The Third Wall,* by Pen Kname."

PENELOPE #1 & #2. (**PENELOPE #1** *is delighted;* **PENELOPE #2** *is unnerved.)* That's me!

PENELOPE #2. I told you our fate is controlled.

SOFIA. It's dated in the future. *(Flips through pages, reading.)* Penelope number one, Anna number one, Penelope number two, Anna number two, Sofia?

PENELOPE #2. Number one and number two?

ANNA #1. These characters are us. We are the characters. Can I have the script?

> **(SOFIA** *hands script to* **ANNA #1,** *who flips through.)*

It has the exact same conversation we've been having since this whole mess started.

PENELOPE #1. Flip to the last page. What does it say?

ANNA #1. It's blank.

PENELOPE #1. *(To* **PENELOPE #2.***)* I told you. The last page isn't written yet because it's our future. We choose our fate.

ANNA #1. The last line that's typed is literally what I'm saying right now, and there's nothing after that.

PENELOPE #2. Has the script changed as we started talking?

ANNA #1. Yes!

> **(PENELOPE #1** *takes the script.)*

SOFIA. Penelope, the script doesn't control us, don't you see? We're generating the dialogue on the page.

ANNA #1. What does this mean?

ANNA #2. My life is a fabulous show that everyone is watching right now?

PENELOPE #1. No.

PENELOPE #2. This means…I finally have an idea for the show I'm going to write!

PENELOPE #1. The show *you're* going to write? *I'm* trying to write a show. *My* pen name is on it.

PENELOPE #2. Is name spelled with a "K" on there?

PENELOPE #1. Yes, but –

PENELOPE #2. That's my pen name too, and I've struggled for way too long to pass this opportunity up.

PENELOPE #1. But –

PENELOPE #2. *I* finally have something interesting to write about. It *will* be a show about me, and I'm going to fix this problem that Anna created in the first place.

PENELOPE #1. You can't take this away from me! This is my show, not yours!

PENELOPE #2. *(Steals the script from* **PENELOPE #1**.*)* Try and stop me.

> *(***PENELOPE #2*** *runs to stage left. She sits and types vigorously. As she is typing, the other characters move backwards as if in reverse. The script is thrown offstage. The computer and wall are restored. Lights flicker, thunder claps. At the end of the chaos, blackout. After applause, if any, stage right is dark; stage left is fully lit.)*

I had an idea…but I can't seem to remember it… This is some serious *déjà vu…*

> *(Inspiration hits. The next lines are said as though reading stage directions. Lights go down. Starts typing.)*

A desk and chair stage right. A wall center stage.

> *(Lights come up stage right.)*

A writer is at the desk concentrating.

> *(***PENELOPE #1*** *rises and sits at desk. Blackout.)*

End of Play

Erin Hyatt as Anna #1 and Kayla Temshiv as Penelope #1 in the Thespian Festival staged reading of *The Third Wall*, by Kim Wong.

Penelope

Phanesia Pharel

Penelope, by Phanesia Pharel of Troupe 3637 at South Dade Senior High School, Homestead, Florida, was presented in a staged reading as part of the Thespian Playworks program at the 2016 Thespian Festival on June 25. Dominic Orlando was director, Jane Barnette served as dramaturg, and Zoila Rodriguez and Abigail Stone served as stage managers. The cast was as follows.

PENELOPE	Sequoiah Hippolyte
ERIS/REGRET	Zainab Barry
SAUL	Duncan Weinland
KLAN MAN/RINGLEADER OF CHAOS	Nicholas C. Pappas
CLUELESS CLOWN	Joe Campbell
JIM CROW	Garrett Ryan
ADVISER OF DREAMS/OWNER OF NIGHTMARES	Evan O'Rourke
PROSTITUTE	Ngakiya Camara
DING DONG	Brody Hawkins
FREEDOM OF SPEECH	Kayla Martinez
CLOCK	Elizabeth Usher
BOOK-KEEPER/SAUL'S MOTHER	Kelly Holstrom
GAEA/THE ORGASM	Aubrey Schoeman
THE CHORUS OF JUDGMENT	Nicholas C. Pappas, Evan O'Rourke, Joe Campbell, Kelly Holstrom, Garrett Ryan
THE CHORUS OF INSECURITY/CHORUS OF DESIRE	Kelly Edwards, Kayla Martinez, Julissa Lopez, Faith Reidinger, Brody Hawkins, Trey McNeil, Aubrey Schoeman

Penelope presents contemporary teenagers in a theatrically heightened universe dealing with racism and sexuality, so it contains language and behavior that might not be suitable for all classrooms or school stages.

CHARACTERS

ERIS – Pronounced EE-riss. Thirty-four. Penelope's mother. A symbol of love and misunderstanding. A prostitute due to the never-evolving social pyramid of Yankeedom. Penelope's standard of beauty.

THE CHORUS OF JUDGMENT – The fully cloaked Ku Klux Klan.

PENELOPE* – Also known as Black Female Number 77. Sixteen. An orphan, hardworking with a sweet soul, but feisty when tested.

KLAN MAN/RINGLEADER OF CHAOS – Owner of the institution, he is the father of Saul. A shadow of hatred. Forty-nine.

THE CHORUS OF INSECURITY – Teenagers. The circus students. Races must be accurate: Native American female, white female, black male, Asian female, Latina female, and one butch lesbian female of any race but black.

ADVISER OF DREAMS/OWNER OF NIGHTMARES* – Thirties. The school counselor.

CLUELESS CLOWN* – Forties. A mean and spastic spirit, complacent clown and teacher.

DING DONG* – Eighteen. Short in height. He pities Clueless Clown (due to his instability) and is only seen in the beginning of the play.

FREEDOM OF SPEECH – Twenties. Personification of the First Amendment.

SAUL* – Seventeen. White male. Son of the Ringleader. Aspiring Ringleader and student in the program. Charming.

BOOK-KEEPER – Forties. Kooky librarian.

CLOCK – Time itself. Any gender. Any age from sixteen to forty.

GAEA – Pronounced GAY-ah. Mature/elderly female. Mother Earth.

GAEA'S MASTER – Forty. American greed and consumption, also known as capitalism. A white businessman with no time to waste.

THE CHORUS OF DESIRE – Chorus members in their teens or early twenties, who represent sexuality.

THE ORGASM – Sixteen. A personified moment of ecstasy and vulnerability.

REGRET – Played by the same actor as Eris. A representation of Penelope's fears.

JIM CROW* – Saul's Grandfather.

SAUL'S MOTHER – Doubles with the Book-Keeper.

PROSTITUTE* – Twenties. Penelope's godmother. A hardworking call girl. Black.

A note on doubling: Most actors can play multiple roles, keeping race in mind, but characters marked with an asterisk (*) should be played by those actors exclusively.

SETTING

Yankeedom. Where the real natives are hidden and the real issues are ignored.

TIME

The present day.

STAGING

The set is a blank canvas. Must have a range of lights and enough open space to hang a tightrope and do aerial. Paint as you please.

TERMS

Noose stick: A representation of the noose which post-slavery discrimination still holds on society.

Yankeedom: The United States of America.

Book Factory: A public library.

Kumbaya: A traditional song representing happy times.

Stomp: A form of art combining polyrhythmic dance, song, and African movement.

Jim, a.k.a. "Jim Crow": a character portrayed by a white man in blackface to create a stereotypically "Negro" persona, popularized in minstrel shows of the 1800s and prominent in the media's attempt to whitewash society. Jim Crow is also a term used to describe the century of segregation and terror between the Civil War/Reconstruction and the Civil Rights era, when "Jim Crow" laws were enacted across the South to restrict the African-American population socially, financially, and politically.

Scene One: A place one in four women will be in their lives

> (**ERIS** *is on her knees center stage, looking up. She hums a sweet but tortured lullaby for a few moments. It is almost as if she is praying. She is dressed in all red.*)

ERIS. I want you to grow baby, okay? I need you to keep our promise. Penelope means faithful. Be faithful to me. Momma Odysseus wants to see you fly. Don't fall. Soar. I'm sorry baby but they are gonna take me away now, I love you.

> (*Spotlights on the* **CHORUS OF JUDGMENT**, *dressed in all-white Ku Klux Klan attire. They circle* **ERIS**; *articles of clothing fly in the air, and we hear cries of agony from the circle. When* **ERIS** *is dead, they go back into formation.* **KLAN MAN** *now carries a long stick attached to a lynching rope, tied to a mason jar full of blood-red liquid, presumably blood.*)

THE CHORUS OF JUDGMENT. A harlot the color of tar.
A harlot grows a fetus in her pussy jar.
A grotesque social, financial, and physical scar.
A harlot has little time before reaching paradise.
Pussy jar fetus she leaves behind.
An orphan left living in the henhouse.
Off you go!
To school to the brothel.
We meet Black Female Number 77 of Yankeedom.

Scene Two: The beginning to the end

(Lights up center stage. **PENELOPE** *is on her knees hurriedly packing items of clothing in a cheap bag.* **KLAN MAN** *follows her with the noose stick, waving it over her head. She never notices him, and neither does anyone else.)*

PENELOPE. Big day! Today will be the day my teachers and peers decide if they hate me. I don't even have the right schedule! I auditioned, received a slot, and bought all the items for the acrobatic strand. WHY ARE ALL MY CLASSES IN CLOWNING?! Momma loved the circus, but she told me school would be a joke, she'd say, "You're going to learn how to do a job from people who haven't even learned how to do theirs." She was so brilliant. Black woman brilliant, it's a whole other level. Thinking about her every day is like Russian roulette, but I know she'd want me to get through for her. I must keep our promise. On the bottom of the ocean floor, my only option is to rise. It will get better. In fact let's start by getting the idiots in the office to fix my schedule.

(Noticing the students near her.)

Excuse me, I need to speak to someone about my schedule. Where should I go?

THE CHORUS OF INSECURITY. Good luck getting some attention!

Don't these matters bring needless frustration?

We like company. Join us. Drugs ease the tension.

*(***PENELOPE*** scoffs at the offer of substance use.)*

But you haven't even tried it! The thrill the sensation.

Do you prefer loneliness? Alone! What a drab situation!

*(***PENELOPE*** changes the subject.)*

PENELOPE. Are you or are you not going to help me find –

THE CHORUS OF INSECURITY. *(Cutting her off.)* Look.

> (**ADVISER OF DREAMS/OWNER OF NIGHTMARES**
> *is seen eating a bag of chocolates near* **PENELOPE**;
> **KLAN MAN** *leaves.* **PENELOPE** *gets up and taps
> the* **ADVISER** *on the shoulder. He sees her and runs.*
> **THE CHORUS OF INSECURITY** *starts laughing.*
> **PENELOPE** *gets tired of the chase and ignores the
> chorus.)*

PENELOPE. *(Exasperated.)* Would you please listen to me?

ADVISER OF DREAMS/OWNER OF NIGHTMARES. DETENTION! RETENTION! SPEAKING OUT WITH DISRESPECT! SO ORIGINAL FOR A DEGENERATE LIKE YOURSELF!

PENELOPE. Excuse me! Adviser of Dreams/Owner of Nightmares, I have been chasing you around all day to fix my schedule, it is entirely wrong! *(Presents class schedule in hand.)*

ADVISER OF DREAMS/OWNER OF NIGHTMARES. *(Grabs it, looks it over and casually rips it in half.)* You will have a new one by the end of the day. It will not be entirely correct. Try to fix it and you will be ignored, lash out and you will face disciplinary action. Would you like a chocolate?

PENELOPE. Fuck you.

ADVISER OF DREAMS/OWNER OF NIGHTMARES. I guess that will be a write-up. Watch out missy, three of those and you will have some nice detention retention. Have a great day. And remember! We are all here to support you.

PENELOPE. So full of it, never met a man in Yankeedom who wasn't a low –

FREEDOM OF SPEECH. Violator! Violator! She violated the constitution! I, Freedom of Speech, only apply to those who are free. You are a piece of chocolate in Yankeedom's factory. Remember, not only can you be replaced, but you can be sold.

PENELOPE. *(Laughs.)* Are you really this backward in thought? The law applies to all of us. Thirteenth Amendment, remember? I am free.

> **(FREEDOM OF SPEECH** *shakes her head and runs offstage.)*

Scene Three: The classroom

(**DING DONG** *bangs a gong.* **THE CHORUS OF INSECURITY** *giggle and make sounds of excitement. They run around the stage doing various circus acts.* **CLUELESS CLOWN** *appears.*)

CLUELESS CLOWN. (*Eccentrically plays around with spastic jumps.*) FRESH MEAT! New peoPle! New seMester! New memOries! Oh, the viGorous adventures we will eXplore! As you can smell, OOPS… I meant "see." I am a clown! But, don't think I can't train you in all of your specialties. I was a part of the under-looked "$5-Please-Come-We-Live-Under-A-Bridge Circus"! (*Beat.*) In regard to the staffing issue… The other teachers for your specialties left on artistic differences when our pay was dropped seventy percent. The way I see it, I live under a bridge so who needs money?

(**CLUELESS CLOWN** *starts crying.* **DING DONG** *offers him his arm as a tissue.* **CLUELESS CLOWN** *blows his nose and instantly feels better.*)

I AM SO SO SO SO SO SO SO SO SO SO SO SO SO, very aroused OOPS I mean excited! If you are experiencing frustration, I recommend masturbation! If you want to air out your dirty laundry, my brain can be your personal washer and dryer! IF you have any questions on what you are learning, please do not ask me. I am an artist, I CANNOT HANDLE QUESTIONS! That will be all. Do what you want for the rest of the class, freedom of speech does apply here. I will say though! Flirtatious glances, sexual innuendos, holding hands, and mouth to mouth on program grounds is highly frowned upon! But not to worry horny horses, we offer protection for you to stay safe.

PENELOPE. (*Laughing to a chorus member.*) So – we can't even kiss but they buy us condoms?

THE CHORUS OF INSECURITY. SILLY CHILD! WHY DO YOU CHOOSE TO SPEAK?

YOUR HUMOR AND APPEARANCE SEEM WEAK!

PENELOPE. My name is Penelo–

(**CLUELESS CLOWN** *gasps in horror.* **CHORUS MEMBERS** *stare at her in disgust.*)

CLUELESS CLOWN. WE DO NOT RECOGNIZE NAMES IN THIS FEROCIOUS AND FINE INSTITUTION! ANY INDIVIDUAL WHO ATTEMPTS TO RECEIVE SPECIAL TREATMENT MAY BE EXPELLED BY THE RINGLEADER!! WHAT IS YOUR SPECIALTY, REBELLIOUS BLACK FEMALE NUMBER 77?

PENELOPE. I belong to the acrobatic strand. I will be a tightrope walker.

(**CLUELESS CLOWN** *whispers into a* **CHORUS MEMBER**'s *ear. They nod and prepare the tightrope again.*)

CLUELESS CLOWN. Show us what you can do.

(**PENELOPE** *climbs onto the rope.* **THE CHORUS OF INSECURITY** *and* **CLUELESS CLOWN** *begin to randomly scream hurtful words like "degenerate," "loser," "worthless."* **PENELOPE** *becomes frustrated and climbs down.*)

PENELOPE. Wow! Thank you very much. No really, THANK YOU. How the hell am I supposed to climb the rope with all of you calling me names?!

CLUELESS CLOWN. THE IMBECILE CAN UNDERSTAND?! Yes! Yes! Yes! That is exactly what I am trying to iterate! This is why we do not have names! If magic fairy dust is sprinkled all over you and somehow you become a successful tightrope walker how can you possibly walk with your fans cheering on your name?! IT'S IMPOSSIBLE!

PENELOPE. Those were insults! My fans wouldn't be insulting me!

CLUELESS CLOWN. With that technique, "chocolate," you'd be surprised.

(**PENELOPE** *is baffled. All characters onstage exit except* **PENELOPE**. **KLAN MAN** *appears with the noose stick and waves it over her head again.*)

PENELOPE. I can't say my name?! This "Ferocious and Fine" institution is facing a drought of common sense. Some clown with no knowledge whatsoever on being a tightrope walker and he is going to train me? Like I'll let the buffoon stop me, I am going to train myself.

(**THE CHORUS OF INSECURITY** *approaches* **PENELOPE**.)

THE CHORUS OF INSECURITY. Perhaps a steady hand?
A quest for knowledge ahead.
Think, contemplate what to demand.

PENELOPE. Thanks!

(*They grab her and hold her up. She does several stunts jumping in the air and stretching her body. When she gets down she feels great.*)

That was amazing. I can't wait to grow with you all and become friends.

(**THE CHORUS OF INSECURITY** *bursts into laughter.*)

THE CHORUS OF INSECURITY. Friends? You are mistaken.
Your spirit will be shaken.
We will not let you win. You are forsaken.

Scene Four: The place where babies come from

> (**PENELOPE** *is very upset. We hear the lullaby from Scene One for a few moments; it abruptly ends as* **SAUL** *walks by, notices her, pulls a piece of chocolate out of his pocket, and gives it to her.* **KLAN MAN** *leaves the stage.*)

SAUL. Hey, I'm Saul. They are fools if you ask me. You are the most talented person here. Other than me... I mean we all have off days, right?

PENELOPE. *(A passive statement that grows.)* Did I ask you? I don't have off days. You don't even know me. It's hard to focus when it's your first day and everyone is calling you names and –

> (**SAUL** *gives her a hug. As they embrace, a* **CHORUS MEMBER** *grabs a microphone and begins to read a poem as they perform the "companion dance." They elegantly dance to the sweet words of the poem.*)

CHORUS MEMBER. Two lions meet
Defying nature
Choices
Choices
Whether or not
To mate
They like to play
They feel gay
One lion is an imbecile
Contemplation of deception
The male feeds onto the woman to feel infinite
Bleeding lions are a hasty sight
Suppose one can find delight.

> (*The* **CHORUS MEMBER** *snaps spastically and walks offstage.* **PENELOPE** *stares into* **SAUL**'*s eyes.*)

PENELOPE. I find the thought of you intoxicating.

SAUL. I loved dancing with you, you aren't making this a fair game.

PENELOPE. I know. You can't be seen giving a degenerate like me affection in public, remember?

SAUL. I am the public. My father is the Ringleader. I own this place.

PENELOPE. So you can do anything you want?

SAUL. Anything.

PENELOPE. Prove it.

(He grabs her for a kiss. They kiss passionately.)

SAUL. You said your name in class, its Pene–. I'm sorry I didn't get all of it.

PENELOPE. Penelope. Penelope Mason.

SAUL. Shhhhh. You are so beautiful. I don't want any sharks to hear. They will eat your pretty little face if they find out.

(The couple freezes. **THE CLOCK** *appears.)*

THE CLOCK.
YOUNG LOVE, SO VAST SO FAST! BRRRIIIINGGGGG!
FOUR MOONS, TWENTY-THREE UNSUPERVISED PLAYDATES,
AND 3,637 MURDERS LATER!

(They unfreeze. Time has passed. The passion between the couple is warmer at this point. This can be shown with a change in lights. **PENELOPE** *kisses* **SAUL.** *)*

PENELOPE. I need a place to study… Don't you have a really nice library at home? If you take me, I'll teach you that fancy French kissing we talked about.

SAUL. As tempting as that sounds, I think the Book Factory would be a lot more peaceful.

PENELOPE. *(Kisses* **SAUL.** *)* If you say so. Thank you. I can always come to you when the air is foggy and I don't understand my surroundings.

SAUL. Me too.

> (**SAUL** *heads off.* **THE CLOCK** *begins to tick. This
> can be done through dance movements or a simple
> "Tick-Tock!" every fifteen seconds or so.* **BOOK-
> KEEPER** *enters.*)

BOOK-KEEPER. How may I help you today?

PENELOPE. I'm looking for some enlightening books.

BOOK-KEEPER. Oh, look! The writing of your people! We
have the best stories… *Woman Overrun by Stress, Sexually
Repressed,* and my favorite, *Death.* You must read them
all!

PENELOPE. Um, you really think I will find these titles
enlightening?

BOOK-KEEPER. Absolutely! I insist, I mean they are right
at your level. But remember, they must be returned in
seven days one hour and three minutes.

PENELOPE. I can definitely handle that. I love reading!

> (**PENELOPE** *starts reading books faster and slower
> based on* **THE CLOCK**'s *ticking or movements.*
> **PENELOPE** *chants out phrases while reading.*)

Hold the right cards.

Keep your mouth shut for love.

True pain resonates the most.

Still overlooked with the breakdowns.

Bland is ugly normal is safer.

Keep those legs closed you'll need to cash it soon.

Suppress, the vulnerable tend to be poor.

Destroy what can't be wrapped around the cranium.

> (**THE CLOCK** *speeds up and freezes.*)

BOOK-KEEPER. You are late!

> (**THE CLOCK** *pushes* **PENELOPE** *on the floor.*)

PENELOPE. But, you said seven days! It's been seven days!

BOOK-KEEPER. I SAID SEVEN DAYS ONE HOUR AND
THREE MINUTES YOU ARE AT SEVEN DAYS ONE
HOUR AND FOUR MINUTES!

PENELOPE. I had to walk here! I walked over a bridge! Can you please understand?

BOOK-KEEPER. Are you trying to bribe me?

PENELOPE. Would you like to be bribed?

BOOK-KEEPER. BANNED! YOU ARE BANNED!

PENELOPE. No please… I need to read more! I can't buy my own…

> (**BOOK-KEEPER** *leaves and* **THE CLOCK** *tauntingly runs offstage.* **SAUL** *appears with chocolate and kisses* **PENELOPE**. **KLAN MAN** *hangs over her with the noose stick.)*

SAUL. I'm sorry you couldn't get any help at the Book Factory. *(Offers her a piece of chocolate.)*

PENELOPE. *(Eating the chocolate.)* It's okay. Do you know of any better places? Why can't I go home with you and read from your library? I mean your dad runs the program, he would understand…it's to help a student.

SAUL. No. I'm sorry baby… My parents are crazy and you don't deserve to be around that. My mom is a joke and my dad hates me. If you want to eat dinner with the masters of passive-aggressive behavior we can definitely eat with my parents.

PENELOPE. Sounds delicious! C'mon. They can't be that bad if they raised you right?

SAUL. Can you just stop? You're crying like a fucking baby. I'm not your "daddy"… It's not my job to take care of you.

PENELOPE. No, you're not my daddy, because he's as good as dead. Thanks. I never called you my dad. I just thought you would want to help me out because that's what you do when you love somebody, but it's fine. You can go just like he did if you want to pretend you love me and speak to me that way.

SAUL. I'm sorry –

> (**PENELOPE** *starts to walk away but remains onstage.)*

PENELOPE. I want to excuse it because I've never felt this
way before.

Scene Five: Unmasking of the pig

(THE CHORUS OF INSECURITY *appears.*
CLUELESS CLOWN *is skipping behind them.*)

CLUELESS CLOWN. AHHHHHHHHHHHHHHHHHHHHHH
HHHHHHHHHHHHHHHHMAzing! You never cease
to amaze me, students. Your level of stupidity is quite
alarming. How will you ever clean up the spills your
parents have left behind… Oh well! All things must
die, including Gaea. Speaking of dying inside, my boss
will be coming in to speak to you today.

SAUL. *(Looks very uncomfortable at this news.)* He always finds
a way to bring me down.

PENELOPE. Wow, Mr. Public, you really think everything is
about you. Newsflash: the school is a mess, if anything
he is here to help us understand how we will train in
our specialties with no teachers. Maybe he hired some
new people!

SAUL. *(Laughing.)* You know what? I'm sorry the man who
has done everything in his power to make me feel
like nothing comes to the only place I feel safe and it
bothers me.

PENELOPE. You are going to be okay, alright?

SAUL. Whatever you say, babycakes.

PENELOPE. Talk to me. Why do you feel safe here?

SAUL. Because they give out free condoms. *(Smiling.)* It's
you. The sun rose and you were the perfect day.

(*He grabs her and they kiss.*)

I really am sorry, okay?

(*She nods.* KLAN MAN *shrugs off his cloak and
hands the noose stick to* SAUL. *He is in a full
ringleader costume. Hence the* RINGLEADER OF
CHAOS.)

RINGLEADER OF CHAOS. The semester is hardly over
and my son is already impregnating his latest flame?

Wonderful. Clown, you never cease to amaze ME. If you weren't the only person trashy enough to accept my shit, I'd toss you out. Students! Do not come to me asking for help, life is a maze…figure it out. You will barely be able to rest with the workload you will be given, but if your body shuts down during a lesson you will be reprimanded. Your class president will handle most of your matters. This is someone who I have been observing for a long time, it sits close to home and it'll be…enlightening to see her in this challenge. She is… Black Female Number 77.

> (**PENELOPE** *looks up, shocked.* **SAUL** *looks unsettled.*)

You have the most potential, Penelope, I see something in you. The world is yours, go take it.

THE CHORUS OF INSECURITY. What about our thoughts?
We are drowning!
We lack beauty.
Poverty loves us and surrounds.
Disappointment in every form.
But we have ideas.
Our perspectives are on opposite wavelengths.
Why am I inhumane?
Why am I cultural vulgarity?
Please help us understand.
Why life is not a friend.

Scene Six: The realization

(All characters disappear except **PENELOPE**, **GAEA**, *and* **GAEA'S MASTER**, *who enter at this time.* **GAEA** *is on her knees, leashed. Her* **MASTER** *is holding her leash.* **GAEA** *speaks to* **PENELOPE**.*)*

PENELOPE. The world is mine… The Ringleader is right. I can do this.

GAEA. Hello! Would you like some water, cancer or AIDS?

*(***GAEA'S MASTER** *coughs.)*

I'm sorry. I failed to mention that I also offer a materialist complex!

PENELOPE. None of those, thank you. I don't want to take anything from the earth. I am here to give you my love and knowledge. I want to transform the earth into a home for us all.

*(***GAEA'S MASTER** *kicks* **GAEA**. **PENELOPE** *gasps and reaches to comfort* **GAEA**, *but her* **MASTER** *raises his hand as if to slap* **PENELOPE**. *She retreats back to her former position.)*

No, no, no… I want to make a difference.

GAEA. Momma can handle the beatings as long as Daddy buys her roses the next day, right?

*(***PENELOPE** *looks confused, unsure if this is a rhetorical question.)*

What if I like the way I am? Hm…what if the seven billion people I nurture are meant to live in cages made of ignorance, greed, and hatred? What if the social order is a lie and global warming is my suicide? Momma's final choice. What if I let these homo sapiens, out of all the creatures that I hold, evolve and survive because I knew you'd all be superficial, materialist, selfish imbeciles that would put me out of my misery? Sell it to a fool who would buy it. There are seven billion people in this world and you think you can make a difference? Good for you.

(Blackout. **GAEA** *and her* **MASTER** *leave the stage.)*

Scene Seven: The scene that leaves parents shriveling up inside

(Lights up. Our lovers are cuddling, **PENELOPE** *crying in* **SAUL***'s arms.* **SAUL** *is not holding the noose stick.)*

PENELOPE. What if Gaea is right? What if everything is a lie and I am a speck in the scope of infinity?! I just want to change things, help people. I want people to know that if they work hard enough they can achieve anything, because baby that's the only reason I'm still here.

SAUL. It's okay… Shhhhh. We all have problems. Don't let them get to you, okay? You are a brilliant, crazy, and sexy woman. And I love you and that means something. Don't sit here and pretend like it doesn't.

PENELOPE. I dare you to say that again.

SAUL. You are brilliant, crazy and sexy. And I love you. Kiss me.

> *(They kiss.* **THE CHORUS OF DESIRE** *appears. They split in two groups and grab the two lovers. The moment is rushed and rough. Articles of clothing fly in the air. The lovers scream out sweet nothings and claims of vulnerability.* **THE ORGASM** *emerges from the circle and the exclamations settle down.)*

THE ORGASM. The moment of ecstasy
Leaves you dreaming of me
Is this heaven
Or hell
I can't tell
I want more
But this is enough
In this moment
You are enough
I know the ceiling above us is falling
But with you
I can be tough.

ERIS/REGRET. *(Picking clothes off the floor.)* Why did you do that… He isn't your slave. There is no stick! If you whip him he can run away. Are you ready for this? Careful is without hurting.

> *(**THE ORGASM** and **REGRET** leave the stage. The lovers emerge from the sexual chaos to different sides on the stage.)*

PENELOPE. I am ready. His love is like sunshine kissing my skin. I would walk across a glass-filled earth naked if he asked me to. He is my nirvana.

SAUL. She's nice. She feels good. I like being around her, I guess you can say she is my happy place. *(Walking over to her.)* You are perfect. I would stay but I can't, I have to see some family so you may not see me for the next few days.

PENELOPE. I'll try to get through my maze without you.

Scene Eight: Childhood memories

(We see **SAUL** *walk into a dining room.* **SAUL'S MOTHER, KLAN MAN,** *and* **JIM CROW** *are all seated at the dining room table.* **SAUL** *reverts to an earlier age, perhaps ten, as he sits.)*

JIM CROW. My boy! How's my grandson doing?

KLAN MAN. We'd be great if only that nigger teacher of his stopped trying to get into grown folks' business.

JIM CROW. My grandson goes to a nigger school! How did this happen?

KLAN MAN. Best school in town wants to hire some niggers and be "liberal," what can I do?

JIM CROW. I can call my friends at the school board and see what I can –

KLAN MAN. No, don't do that. I'll deal with the bitch myself. Saul did something nasty one day and so I gave him a little spanking. The next day I get a call from that nigger trying to tell me how to take care of my kid!

JIM CROW. That's the thing with them, you give 'em a little freedom and they start acting like they own the damn place. Tryna take everything away from you!

SAUL. Who are you talking about, Gramps?

KLAN MAN. Stay out of adult conver–

JIM CROW. That's all right. It's time he knows. I don't trust that his mind is clear. Son, what's the difference between a black man and a white man?

SAUL. The color of skin?

JIM CROW. Now that's what they teaching you kids in school? Fillin' ya heads with nonsense? Saul, the truth is, the difference between a white man and a black man is one is smart and the other is as good as a monkey. The blacks were being tools of the devil in Africa, and we did what good Christians always do, we put 'em to work. The Church gave us money for boats and we took 'em and whipped 'em into shape. Then some got smarter, you know? Watching us. They rebelled, the Confederates were strong but we lost that battle but we still got a war, Saul! We can't let them play us! You got to hold 'em down! You got to let them animals get treated like the vermin they are! YOU CAN'T FAIL ME! WE HAVE COME SO FAR!

SAUL. *(Crying.)* I'm sorry Gramps. I'm so sorry... I didn't mean to be nice to them, I didn't know!

SAUL'S MOTHER. Stop it Jim! He's just a child.

KLAN MAN. *(Slaps SAUL'S MOTHER.)* Stupid bitch! SHUT YOUR MOUTH! DON'T SPEAK TO MY FATHER THAT WAY –

SAUL. *(Crying.)* GRAMPS MAKE IT STOP! PLEASE!

> (**KLAN MAN** *drags* **SAUL'S MOTHER** *offstage.* **JIM CROW** *takes* **SAUL** *by the hand.*)

JIM CROW. It's okay, let me show you the truth.

> *(They spin and are surrounded by six white people in blackface. They make monkey sounds and try to attack* **SAUL**.*)*

MONKEY. Welcome to the brothel, honey! I'm going to show you our finest gem...Penelope.

> (**SAUL** *looks around nervously while the* **MONKEYS** *gang up, ad-libbing, "You got the fever? You wanna get nasty in the jungle?"* **SAUL** *starts crying as the stress of his parents and the anxiety of race issues overwhelm him.*)

JIM CROW. You can't let me down! We have come too far!

> (**JIM CROW** *grabs a gun and shoots one of the nasty* **MONKEYS**, *dispersing them.*)

SAUL. Thank you, Gramps.

JIM CROW. You can call me Jim Crow.

> *(He walks offstage.* **SAUL** *is older now. We see him glance at* **PENELOPE**, *this is a flashback to when they said goodbye.*)

SAUL. What have I done?

Scene Nine: The breaking point

>(**PENELOPE** *dances happily. She is singing the lullaby hummed at the beginning of the play. Everyone fades away. She lies down on the floor, smiling, as if she is staring at stars. Next to her* **THE CHORUS OF INSECURITY** *suddenly emerges, ideally from trapdoors in the stage floor, wearing school apparel.* **PENELOPE** *screams.*)

PENELOPE. Are you guys trying to jump me? Look, I'm broke, let's look through my wallet together. It would honestly be magic if we found anything in there.

WHITE FEMALE 3. I am sorry. We need you. This ship is sinking and the captain needs to do something. We haven't been learning anything real. We are killing our bodies with malnutrition and lack of sleep. I haven't felt happy in months.

ASIAN FEMALE 89. You are class president.

PENELOPE. *(Dramatic gasp.)* Thank you for reminding me. I am aware. And I am also aware that I have no power on this ship. How can you come to me for help after all the crap you've put me through? Are you delusional?

NATIVE AMERICAN FEMALE 45. You don't understand. If you don't figure it out –

PENELOPE. You forget who the hell you're talking to. I'm president of this circus. So if you find a file of yours missing or can't get lunch or miss an opportunity, I promise it's my doing. You tried to shake my spirit and I'm gonna make sure *your* life is hell. And if you have a problem with that, you can talk to my boyfriend whose father owns this fine institution.

BLACK MALE 8. You don't mean that.

PENELOPE. Excuse me?

BLACK MALE 8. Don't let his love fool you. You are still like me. I know you're drowning too. There's so much happening all at once I don't know what to decide who to reach out to, no one I meet seems to really be there.

LESBIAN 57. Papa see my beauty!

NATIVE AMERICAN FEMALE 45. Where is the balance?

ASIAN FEMALE 89. I want to belong.

LATINA FEMALE 87. I want to understand.

WHITE FEMALE 3. I want to be understood.

BLACK MALE 8. I want Penelope to be Penelope.

> *(There is an awkward pause. The chocolate acquaintances stare into each other's eyes.)*

PENELOPE. You didn't have to make a scene. I'll help. You never made me feel welcome, but no one deserves to feel the way we do. Who knows what we could've accomplished if we had worked together? As for the other half of me, if he is changing me it is for the better. I'll let you guys know about my game plan soon.

BLACK MALE 8. Thank you, Penelope.

> *(Flabbergasted, she leaves. She walks over to where the **RINGLEADER** has been seated at a desk. He is sitting, going through paperwork.)*

PENELOPE. Hi! How are you? Are you busy? I've been meaning to speak to you about my class and ways we can improve the program!

RINGLEADER. Don't worry about my work, there will always be more. Enlighten me.

PENELOPE. Okay, thank you. A lot of students are having issues with getting enough rest to keep up with the program. Perhaps, if we have fewer days or based our grades on effort we could improve the standards?

RINGLEADER. If I let you kids go home more, the donkeys and elephants will come after me. I don't need that headache.

PENELOPE. But the elephants and donkeys are our animals! They are supposed to be working for us. For the people right? Children are people! We deserve to have a say in the way we are taught!

RINGLEADER. And you do. Every school has overworked, politically unattractive student council officers who try their hardest to get their point across. They never do because you are just a classless attraction in Yankeedom's games. When I found out my son was "getting it on" with a dirty nigger from the brothel I wanted to squash you, but this is so much better. You are a political sensation! Smart niggers are the trend of the season! You seem to have a brain and all the circuses think my son such a nice, progressive guy. His ability to overlook your black problem is wonderful. Once he becomes Ringleader to a great circus, he can find a suitable wife, but for now you will do.

PENELOPE. He was right. You're a pig. But he loves me. We are infinite. And I will make a difference. We are going to be together. Whether you like it or not.

(All characters on stage freeze. A battered yet beautiful woman appears.)

PROSTITUTE. I have a beautiful goddaughter. She is smart. I don't know how but she is so close to doing the things she always dreamed of. It's killing her though. I see her come home at ten and she stays up 'til four then she wakes up at six and starts the cycle all over again. She never has time to eat and she never has time to relax. And that boy, he isn't good for her. I know he's not. He won't even walk into the brothel and say hi. That's a part of Penelope. She is a product of this and Saul can't ignore that. I wish she would quit all of this. She's too young, it's too much for her. I want her to sleep and work with us here at the brothel. This is where she belongs. Her mother would be proud of her though, and I think that's why she is still doing it. It's been three years since Eris died and Penelope has been doing well, that is, before she joined the program. I am trying to be a good godmother and fill Eris's slot but I know I don't understand Penelope.

>(*Noticing the* **RINGLEADER**. *Her glance unfreezes him and he begins to admire her.*)

Like what you see?

RINGLEADER. Depends how much you'll show me.

PROSTITUTE. Anything you want.

RINGLEADER. How much do you want?

PROSTITUTE. One hundred an hour but if I am good, you have to promise me another date. I like to leave my clients satisfied.

>(*He smiles and grabs her waist. She kisses his neck and walks offstage with him.*)

Right this way sir…

Scene Ten: The classroom

> (*The* **CHORUS OF INSECURITY** *are seen speaking to* **PENELOPE**; *they are planning the rebellion.* **SAUL** *appears with* **CLUELESS CLOWN**, *who looks happier than ever.* **SAUL** *appears suspicious and makes no attempts to speak to* **PENELOPE**.)

CLUELESS CLOWN. I am going to die in ten years! I am going to die in ten years! I am going to die in ten years! IT'S HAPPENING, I AM OFFICIALLY RETIRING!

> (**CLUELESS CLOWN** *begins to cry happy tears.* **LESBIAN 57** *tries to comfort him, thinking he is having a breakdown, and he pushes her off.*)

I am stupendous! I need no pity! This is the greatest moment of my life! WITH THE FIVE QUARTERS THEY ARE GOING TO GIVE ME, I CAN MOVE TO A BRIDGE IN THE CITY!

> (*The* **STUDENTS** *are unsure how to react.*)

OKAY! SINCE TODAY IS MY LAST DAY…you are in for a treat. I will be completely honest with the top kids on their "futures" and then I will teach you basic skills and then we can leave early!!

> (*The* **STUDENTS** *clap and cheer.* **THE CHORUS OF INSECURITY** *assembles into a line. The* **CLOWN** *calls each one forth and gives his advice.*)

Saul, you privileged son of a bitch! You will most likely inherit this chaos off your father which is going to be FUN FUN to watch. Asian number 89, try to learn how to juggle the expectations and realities. Latina number 87, I can see you unicycling! …Your way back over the border that is.

LATINA FEMALE 87. I was born in Kansas!

CLUELESS CLOWN. THAT SHOULD BE IT! NOW TO MY WATERED-DOWN TEACHING!

PENELOPE. Sir, you skipped over me!

CLUELESS CLOWN. You are an ant in a beehive. I don't know what to say to you.

PENELOPE. But I am the hardest-working person here?! Have you not noticed anything I have done this year?!

CLUELESS CLOWN. Let me think… Didn't you stumble on the tightrope…the first day of school?

PENELOPE. And I organized all our activities! Impressed the guest speakers! And –

CLUELESS CLOWN. Look. We really have to move on. When I finish my lesson you can go to your counselor.

> *(***CLUELESS CLOWN*** *grabs a trumpet, plays off-key, and creates silence. What happens next is very visual and should be silent. The* **STUDENTS** *should appear to be trying their best and keeping up with the basic instruction, but all movements must seem robotic.* **CLUELESS CLOWN** *will demonstrate various movements and each* **STUDENT** *will copy. This should go on for no more than one minute. Finally* **CLUELESS CLOWN** *will somersault, the* **STUDENTS** *will not follow that movement, and it will represent the end of the lesson.* **STUDENTS** *are silent and an aura of aggravation fills the room.)*
>
> *(***PENELOPE*** *walks off to see the* **ADVISER***; he seems stressed as he throws the papers in his hands and screams.)*

PENELOPE. Are you okay?

ADVISER OF DREAMS/OWNER OF NIGHTMARES. NO I'm not "okay," three hundred people to guard and personally handle! I don't even have time to brush my own teeth. They screw you kids over too. No wonder Yankeedom is ending.

PENELOPE. I want to get out! I don't know what to do! I just want to be an individual and no one will let me!

ADVISER OF DREAMS/OWNER OF NIGHTMARES. We are like slaves picking cotton for a piece of the dirt and a constant whipping from the system. We didn't ask for this, hell the system didn't even ask to be a piece of shit. But it is what it is. Kid, you're never getting out. All you can do is give them the middle finger before you get shipped off to the next plantation. Show them originality. Sometimes the master tries to learn from the slave, because secretly they want to be different. All you can do is try. Finals are coming up, give them a show.

Scene Eleven: The rebellion

> (**THE CHORUS OF INSECURITY** *launches some actors into an aerial number. While the aerial act is going on the* **CHORUS MEMBERS** *sing and dance as they exclaim, "A show! What a whimsical wondrous event!"* **PENELOPE** *comes down from her aerial and is grabbed and slapped by* **SAUL**. *He is holding the noose stick.* **PENELOPE** *notices the noose stick for the first time.*)

SAUL. What is wrong with you? You bitch. How could you do this to me, can you not behave for just one damn second?

PENELOPE. How dare you, what could I ever do to make you treat me this way? You aren't the man I fell in love with. You are a dog. I didn't do anything to you, are you mad that I run the show? That your own daddy couldn't see you over me? How pathetic. If you ever lay your hand on a woman again I will show you how a bitch kills.

SAUL. Shut that mouth, shut that ugly mouth. You think that any circus is gonna want me to be their ringleader when I can't even control my nigger? This little rebellion is over.

PENELOPE. No it's not, but we are. This is over. You began to drift a long time ago, I tried to warn you, but you were on the far side of the moon. Bring the entire zoo, the elephants and donkeys are going to be extinct when I'm done here.

> (**PENELOPE** *does a somersault and begins to announce the show.*)

Hello! My name is Penelope! And –

> (*She notices* **BLACK MALE 8** *smiling at her. She pauses, smiles, and walks up to* **LESBIAN 57**. *She kisses her provocatively.*)

Enjoy the show.

(The **CHORUS** *begins to do an intense and compelling stomp number, using sticks, trash can lids, cans, and other objects for percussion. The lights should be sparkling and beautiful.* **PENELOPE** *pirouettes and taps the stick seven times. A crescendo.)*

A final is a summary of what you have learned. This is what we have taken from this fine institution.

LESBIAN 57. *(Making crude slurping sound, as a bully might imitate oral sex, while shaking a trash bag.)* I am twice as likely to be physically assaulted, kicked or shoved at school.

NATIVE AMERICAN FEMALE 45. *(Making stereotypical "Indian" war whoops while banging on the bottom of a trash can.)* The early bird does not always get the worm.

ASIAN FEMALE 89. *(Performing karate while holding sticks.)* There is no such thing as a good stereotype.

WHITE FEMALE 3. *(Fanning herself and singing lightly with the trash can top.)* One in four women will be sexually assaulted in their lifetimes.

BLACK MALE 8. *(Making an intricate beat with sticks.)* My life does not matter.

LATINA FEMALE 87. *(Sultry dancing with a trash bag.)* It's hard to unicycle without a wheel.

SAUL. *(Off to the side. He is not in the performance.)* Black women are a pain in the ass.

(The **CHORUS** *continues making their various beats to a tempo that showcases each one. They dance, jump, and stomp as they rotate the different items. The* **CHORUS** *repeats this phrase as they place the tightrope up and carry* **PENELOPE** *to the tightrope: "If all lives matter then why doesn't mine." Off to the side,* **SAUL** *angrily taunts* **PENELOPE** *with the noose stick. Their love flashes before her eyes.* **PENELOPE** *is on the tightrope; she appears in a state beyond stress, it is almost as*

if she is having an anxiety attack. She begins to hallucinate and see her mother.)

ERIS. Penelope! You did it! You are walking on the tightrope! I'm so proud of you.

PENELOPE. What the hell? Momma is that you? It's happened, I've officially lost my mind. Wherever you are, Momma. I'm so sorry. I tried my best. I tried to show them. I spoke well, I did my work, and I went above and beyond. But they ignored me. And I fell in love, it was insanity.

ERIS. It's okay, don't worry. You are on the right track. You just have to keep going! You fell in love? What the hell? I mean you are pretty, but I mean women like us can never find water in this desert. I'm so proud of you.

PENELOPE. You shouldn't be. I let someone in. And he was terrible…he hit me, he made me feel dirty and called me a nigger. He's the nigger, they are all niggers. Ignorant, stupid, and…

(Begins to lose balance.) You are the smartest person I ever met. You understood individuality and depth. These people just want more meat to butcher.

ERIS. Who cares? Who cares if they don't want to see you swim, darling they are going to want you to drown! You are brown, and poor, and smart. This world isn't going to love you. But you have to love yourself enough to swim!

PENELOPE. No. If I can't even breathe or be accepted into his performers' program, how am I going to do it in the real world? I'm drowning, and I want to see you, but for more than five minutes. Mom, I'm depleted.

ERIS. No I won't let you! You are too smart. Penelope means faithful! Remember baby! Keep our promise!

PENELOPE. Momma. There are excuses and then there are reasons. What is intelligence? We are all impaired in one aspect.

CLUELESS CLOWN. YOU'RE ALL CLUELESS IDIOTS AND SO AM I!

*(Throws piece of chocolate at **PENELOPE**.)*

PENELOPE. There is the opportunity to develop in which some are not fortunate enough to achieve.

SAUL. I am the public. Black women are a pain in the ass.

*(Throws piece of chocolate at **PENELOPE**.)*

PENELOPE. Momma I wish my lover was true so that I could've held onto him forever, because he kept me afloat. You gave me hope and helped fuel the fire inside me, but you are gone and now I feel so alone.

BLACK MALE 8. Are you alone, doll face?

PENELOPE. If this chaotic system had room for me then I would stay.

KLAN MAN. The world is yours, go take it.

*(Throws piece of chocolate at **PENELOPE**.)*

PENELOPE. I lied and ruined myself. I love you more than the word describes, Momma, I am sorry. But I need to go now. I don't have time, space or even a decent place to sleep. I am an ant in a beehive and I –

(She falls off the tightrope. Curtain closes.)

End of Play

Sequoiah Hippolyte in the title role of *Penelope,* by Phanesia Pharel, backed by The Chorus of Judgment in the Thespian Festival staged reading.